Arjun's PENANCE

A contemporary romance novel by

SUNDARI VENKATRAMAN

*Love,
Sundari*

FLAMING SUN

Notion Press Media Pvt Ltd
No. 50, Chettiyar Agaram Main Road,
Vanagaram, Chennai, Tamil Nadu – 600 095

First Published by Flaming Sun 2020
Printed & Distributed by Notion Press
Copyright © Sundari Venkatraman 2020 & 2023
All Rights Reserved.

ISBN 979-8-89186-977-6

Edited by: The Book Club Editorial Panel
Cover Illustration: Unaiza Merchant

Ten years! Arjun had lived the life of penance for ten years, staying completely away from women. He had placed his heart on deep freeze mode and refused to let it thaw. And to be fair, there had been no reason for it to soften up. He had simply refused to interact with women.

There were people who sniggered behind his back, calling him a Buddha. Arjun was even aware of it. Not that he cared.

It was with great difficulty he had achieved this state of calm, wrapping himself in a cocoon which kept women at bay. He didn't want to depend on the female species for anything. The only woman he trusted was his mother. Wasn't it a good thing he wasn't dependent on her for anything? And Anjali would never demand anything from her son, at least nothing he wouldn't want to give her.

But today, it looked like his very foundation, the comfort zone which he had settled into for over a decade, was shaken.

Kiara!

The young lady who had walked into his office today had been like a breath of fresh air. In one visit, she had somehow managed to tear through the cobwebs of his past and reached to his inner core. So much so that Arjun felt threatened.

All it had taken was the soft touch of her feminine hand!

ABOUT THE AUTHOR

Sundari Venkatraman is an Indie Author who has 65 books to her credit. These books have consistently featured in the Top 100 Bestseller Lists on Amazon Kindle, in both romance as well as Asian Drama categories. Her latest hot romances have all been on #1 Bestseller slot in Amazon India for over a month.

ARJUN'S PENANCE is a hot romance and a sequel to An Autograph for Anjali; though it can be read as a standalone novel. This kindle book remained in #1 Bestseller position on Amazon India for three months from its release.

Even as a child, Sundari absolutely loved the 'lived happily ever after' syndrome and she grew up on a steady diet of fairy tales, Phantom comics and Mandrake comics. It was always about good triumphing over evil and a happy ending after the protagonists surmounted all unexpected obstacles.

Once she entered her teens, Sundari switched her loyalties from fairy tales to Mills & Boon. While she loved reading both, she kept visualising what would have happened if there were similar situations happening in India; to local heroes and heroines. And of course, the joy of vanquishing the ubiquitous evil villains! Her imagination soared and she happily ensconced herself in a rosy romantic cocoon for many years.

Then came the writing—a true bolt from the blue! And Sundari Venkatraman has never looked back.

Books by Sundari Venkatraman

Standalone novels
The Malhotra Bride
Meghna
The Madras Affair
An Autograph for Anjali
Twin Torment
Finding Anya
Mr. Perfect
Man Friday
Her Prince Charming
Love in Agartha
Arjun's Penance
The Floundering Author
Ryan Finds a Bride
Tinder Loving Care
Shaan Gets Hitched
For Better or For Worse
Love… No Conditions Asked

Collection of shorts
Matches Made in Heaven
Tales of Sunshine

Marriages Made in India Series
#1 The Runaway Bridegroom
#2 Her Smitten Husband
#3 His Drunken Wife
#4 Her Secret Husband
#5 The Casanova's Wife
#6 Her Bohemian Husband

The Bansal Legacy Trilogy
#1 Simha International
#2 Rose Garden International
#3 Maharaja International

The Thakore Royals Trilogy
#1 The Marriage Predicament
#2 Tied in Knots
#3 The Wooing of the Shrew

The Groom Series Trilogy
#1 Groomnapped
#2 Gobsmacked
#3 Grounded

Written in the Stars Series
#1 Scorpio Superstar
#2 Leo's Desire
#3 Taurus Temptation
#4 Virgo's Krush
#5 Libra's Flame

Arora Iyers Trilogy
#1 Once Bitten Twice Lucky
#2 Heartthrob
#3 Call of the Heart

Dashavatar (Indian Mythology)
MATSYA: The First Avatar
KURMA: The Second Avatar
VARAHA: The Third Avatar
NARASIMHA: The Fourth Avatar
VAMANA: The Fifth Avatar
PARASHURAMA: The Sixth Avatar

**The Princess Series
(Historical Romance)**
#1 The Passionate Princess
#2 The Rebel Princess

The Writer's Toolkit (Non-fiction)
Publishing Your Book on Amazon KDP

Bollywood Bros Trilogy
#1 Sing For Me
#2 Dance With Me

Romantic Shorts
#1 *Chahti Hoon Tumhe*
#2 Beauty is but Skin Deep
#3 Madeinheaven.com
#4 An Arranged Match
#5 The Reluctant Bride
#6 *Shweta ka Swayamvar*
#7 Papa's Girl
#8 Red Rose Dating Agency
#9 Rahat Mili
#10 Reema's Matchmakers
#11 The Matchmaker's Dream

PROLOGUE

"Anjali, sweetheart!" Parth's voice was gruff over the phone.

"Parth, I've missed you." Anjali confessed. She was home in Mumbai while he—her second husband whom she adored—was in faraway London.

"As I have you. How did your book launch go? I feel so terrible missing it."

"It was really good. So, tell me, when are you returning home?"

"I've booked you on a flight to London tonight. Pack as fast as you can and get to the airport in, say, six hours."

Anjali gurgled with laughter, excitement choking her throat. It was less than a year since their marriage and she was more in love with Parth than ever. "Done. Let me call Sita and ask her to take care of Sam." Sita used to be the cook at the Mathurs' home when Anjali lived there with her first husband—now deceased—Jayant and their son Arjun. Nowadays, the cook was semi-retired and lived in a small flat of her own not far from Hiranandani Gardens in Powai, all thanks to Arjun's generosity. She was only too happy to take care of Anjali's Tomcat Sam whenever the latter and her husband had to travel.

"I'll be waiting for you at Heathrow. Until then, my sweetheart." He paused before saying in a passionate whisper, "I love you, Anjali."

"Can't wait to meet you, my Parth. I love you too."

Parth didn't tell his wife that he had taken up residence at Arjun's London apartment, taking care of his stepson who had just been discharged from hospital. Between the two of them, Parth and Arjun had decided to not tell Anjali too much about what had happened, but only the bare details.

Anjali was absolutely beat when she landed at Heathrow the next morning local time 6:55 AM. She fell into Parth's waiting arms when she finally got out of the airport after completing all the formalities.

Pressing his lips to her forehead, Parth held her close to his side as he guided her out of the airport and into the waiting chauffer-driven car.

Anjali got inside and placed her head on Parth's shoulder the moment he settled beside her, a soft smile on her lips. "Did you get a chance to meet Arjun?"

"I'm staying with him. And that's where we are heading now."

"Oh!" There was surprise on Anjali's face. "Is Jane not there?" Arjun was in a live-in relationship with Jane McKenzie who was from Scotland. She was not only his college mate, but the love of his life.

"No." Parth sighed, long and loud.

"What's wrong, Parth?" Anjali moved away from him to look into his silver gaze.

"Why do you think something's wrong?" He raised an eyebrow as he drank in her lovely features.

"Parth!"

He sighed again. "I think Arjun would want to tell you himself."

"Have they broken up?" Anjali's voice was a strained whisper. She knew how much her son loved Jane.

Parth shook his head, turning away to look out of the window.

It wasn't like her husband to not meet her gaze. Placing a hand on his shoulder, Anjali said, "Parth, I want you to tell me."

He turned back to look at her. "Jane died in an accident, Anjali. Arjun's heartbroken."

Ten years later…

As Managing Director of the Mathur Group of Industries, thirty-year-old Arjun had a finger in many pies. The company had come a long way from his father's days. While Jayant had set up the company as a single unit, producing and marketing designer luggage, Arjun had expanded his father's multi-million legacy by adding a variety other leather products; tying up with major fashion brands from around the globe. The company had six factories spread across North India while it's Research and Development Department was on par with similar ones across the world.

All this, he had done remotely while studying at Kingston University, completing both his graduation and post-graduation before gaining experience in similar industries in both the UK and the USA. Arjun had literally slogged during those years, working two shifts to gain as much knowledge and experience as was possible in the span of seven years.

Even during that period, he had been remotely running the company, though many people on the board as well as in the company's employ, weren't aware of it.

Shiamak Trivedi, the oldest member on the board of directors, was left in charge of running the company after Jayant Mathur passed away. Having been on the board since the very inception of Mathur Industries when Jayant set it up, Shiamak knew the workings like the back of his own hand. He was also loyal to the Mathurs and treated Arjun like a grandson. The old man was only too happy to carry out every instruction given him by Arjun Mathur.

Now, it was three years since Arjun had returned to Mumbai to take over the reins of his father's legacy which had grown by leaps and bounds.

And in those years, Arjun had become renowned in the industry for his ruthless business tactics. He was as different from the compassionate young man he had been a dozen years ago, at the time when his father was murdered.

Arjun Mathur was chairing a board meeting now. Leaning back in his chair at the head of the table, a fist under his chin while his gaze was trained on the notepad in front of him, Arjun was listening to Kirit Patel, the director of finance, as he spoke about the budget for the coming financial year.

Kirit, in turn, was fuming. At fifty-seven, he didn't care for the idea of being answerable to this young puppy. Until Arjun came on board, it hadn't been difficult pulling the wool over Shiamak Trivedi's eyes, a managing director in his eighties. Kirit could not only get away with doing as little work as possible, but he had even managed to swindle the company of crores of rupees. After all, what use was the company if it couldn't pay for the benefits of its management, especially the finance director?

But with Arjun in the Managing Director's chair, life had become too difficult. Kirit hadn't been able to get extra money out, at least not as much as he used to. And over and above that, he had been forced to work his butt off.

Maybe Arjun would also go the same way as his father, murdered in his bed at an even younger age. For Kirit knew how many people in the office hated the MD's guts. From the time Arjun personally took the reins in his hand, the company had not only expanded and more job opportunities created, it had also been time for many heads to roll. And Arjun had personally seen to it.

Suddenly, Arjun lifted a hand to stop Kirit in mid-sentence. "Listen, Kirit, I'll grant you an extra thirty million rupees for the coming year." Even as the older man's face lit up in greed, Arjun dropped the bomb, "What I need from you is a new budget, tighter than what you have now, including the welfare of a children's home we have adopted recently. And by the way, there are about fifteen hundred children from the ages of zero to fourteen in this home. This is our CSR project for the coming year. The children need food, clothes, schooling, plus caretakers. The structure they are living in is dilapidated, to say the least. We need to shift them to a better place with a large compound, maybe about five acres. Right now, they live in Kurla with twenty children to every hundred square-foot space. And the change needs to be incorporated ASAP, by the second week of February. You…"

Flabbergast, Kirit protested loudly, "But… but Arjun, that's less than a month away. Simply not possible. I…"

"In that case, I'll have to ask Mudit Trivedi to take over." Not waiting for the stuttering Kirit to speak further, Arjun turned to his right and said, "What do you think, Mudit? Will you be able to give me a budget in three days?"

Mudit, at thirty-one, had come on board only after Arjun had taken over as the MD and was as honest as they came. Shiamak Trivedi was his grandfather and Mudit had taken the older man's place on the board after he retired. Now, Mudit nodded. "Sure. I've already made a note of your requirements, Arjun. I can present the budget to you the day after tomorrow."

"All in favour of Mudit Trivedi for finance director?" Arjun counted the raised hands before saying, "We have fifteen votes. And those against the motion?" Five directors including Kirit raised their hands. "It's a clean sweep. Kirit, see that you handover all the files to Mudit immediately. And with this, I declare the meeting closed."

Not waiting for the others to say anything, Arjun got up from his chair and left the board room.

Kirit glared at Arjun's retreating back with hatred in his eyes. If looks could kill, the managing director of the Mathur Group of Industries would have fallen down dead before he crossed the threshold out of the room.

"Hello, Mom." Arjun's voice was so gentle that anyone hearing him would never have believed it was the same man who had chucked Kirit Patel from his position in the company in the matter of minutes and a couple of sharp moves. Arjun adored his mother, Anjali and his step-father, Parth; the only two people he also trusted in the whole world. He would lay down his life for either of them.

"Arjun! You're too busy nowadays. I've almost forgotten your face," said Anjali teasingly.

"Hahaha! Come on, Mom. Didn't we meet for dinner the week before last? How come I recall your face with crystal clarity?"

"Very funny, young man. I want you to come over for dinner tonight."

"What's the occasion?" Arjun didn't want to upset his parent, but he simply wasn't in the mood to socialise. And the love they shared—his mother and stepfather—made him feel envious. It wasn't as if they piled on the affection publicly. But they obviously couldn't help themselves with the looks and touches they shared.

It was not as if Arjun suffered from a dearth of feminine attention. More than average height at six feet, three inches and looks acquired from the best of both his parents' genes, Arjun was stunningly handsome. Just turned thirty a few months back and heading a corporate; his personal worth running into a few billions, Arjun was definitely a matrimonial catch drooled over by many young women as well as their mammas. But the problem was that Arjun had sworn off women. He wanted no one as his partner after the experience with Jane. It was as if he had locked his heart and thrown away the key.

"Arjun! Do you need an occasion to come home for dinner? Parth is making something special. We want you here by eight. And no excuses. I'll see you then. Bye."

Arjun wanted to laugh when he heard the click which told him that his mother had cut the call. Shaking his head, he turned to his laptop to continue typing. Wasn't it a good thing they stayed in the same compound at Hiranandani Gardens in Powai? Arjun continued to live on the tenth floor of *Helios*, in the apartment his father had bought when Arjun had been eight years old. While many people—both friends and relatives—had advised him to sell the apartment as his father had been murdered there, Arjun hadn't listened to anyone. He had loved his father and had only had happy times in his home. After performing a few *havans*, Arjun had retained his home, returning to it a couple of weeks every year during his time abroad before settling down there after he finally moved back home to Mumbai.

Arjun left work at seven that evening—way earlier than his usual time—driving home in his sleek, black

BMW. He didn't bother to speak to his employees when he left the office, lifting a hand when some of them called out to wish him a nice weekend, the expression on his face as aloof as always. It was rare indeed when Arjun smiled.

It was a few minutes after eight when he rang the doorbell to the penthouse at *Olympus*, a bouquet of exotic flowers for his mother and a bottle of Johnny Walker Blue Label whiskey for Parth.

"Arjun!" Anjali took her son's hand and pulled him into the apartment before hugging him. "Are these for me? Beautiful," she gushed, taking the flowers from his hand.

Kissing her cheek, Arjun said, "I love you, Mom. You're looking good." At almost fifty, Anjali glowed with the inner light of a much-loved woman. There were no traces of the clinical depression she had suffered from many years ago, before Parth.

"And I love you, son. How have you been?" She moved away to look at her only offspring up and down.

"Just great," said Arjun with a smile which didn't reflect in his big, brown eyes which were exactly like hers.

Parth walked into the living room, a wide smile on his face. "Hey Buddy! Good to see you." He hugged Arjun.

"Parth! How have you been?" Arjun offered the whiskey to his stepfather.

"All good. And you? Appreciate this," responded Parth, accepting the bottle.

An inadvertent sigh emerged from Arjun before he could stop himself. Shrugging, he said, "I'm good."

Parth looked into Arjun's eyes, his silver gaze shrewd. He knew that Arjun hadn't forgotten Jane, not one little bit. It was just sad that the younger man was only punishing himself, living the life of a recluse. The cheerful boy he had befriended all those years ago seemed to have disappeared forever.

"What will you have to drink?" asked Parth, walking over to the spacious bar on the left-hand side corner of the living room.

"I'll have a long island iced tea," said Arjun, a glimmer of a smile on his face. His stepfather was not just an amazing cook, but also made some excellent cocktails. "Would you like the same, Mom?" Arjun went to sit next to her on the sofa.

"Yeah, sure. Parth, go light on the alcohol for me." Anjali looked towards her husband with a wide smile. The first time she had had one of his cocktails, she had got drunk after the first few sips.

"You bet," said Parth, grinning right back as he mixed the drinks. Soon, he brought over two tall glasses and handed over the lighter drink to his wife before giving Arjun the stronger one. He returned to get his own drink, a screwdriver cocktail, before touching the tip of his glass to the others', saying, "Cheers!"

"Cheers!" chorused Anjali and Arjun before sipping from their glasses.

There was *bhel puri* and *sev puri* on the menu, along with *fried rice* and *paneer chilli in gravy*. Arjun binged on the *chaat* items. "These are simply too good, Parth."

"Glad to know," said Parth, munching on some roasted peanuts. "So, what's happening at work? You had a directors' meeting today, right?"

Arjun gave his stepfather a devilish grin, his face transforming for a few seconds. "I ousted Kirit Patel from his position as finance director in the company. I am sure the bastard has been swindling from us for a while. And it's so damn difficult to get proof since he had a tight hold over the whole department all this long. But not any longer. Mudit Trivedi is our finance director from now. He's already on Kirit's case."

Anjali shook her head. "Are you sure, Arjun? Kirit Patel is callous. I don't want him to harm you or your company in some way."

"Today, Mom, your son has the reputation of being the most ruthless businessman in India." Arjun lifted his eyebrow at Parth, seeking his affirmation.

"That's right, Anjali. Arjun does have a reputation." Parth couldn't help but feel sad as he agreed to Arjun's claim. The boy he had known used to be one of the most compassionate human beings. But not so these days. While Arjun was hard-headed in his business, he had no private life at all. He couldn't help wondering what Arjun did in his free time. Parth used to be Arjun's confidante once upon a time. But not since Jane's death. The heartbreak seemed to have aged Arjun, as well as turned him a hundred per cent cynical overnight.

Anjali refused to believe either man's words. They must be fooling her. She knew her son. He was an adorable young man who had a heart of gold. If he was confident of dealing with the likes of Kirit Patel, wasn't it a good thing?

"And this Mudit?" she asked, "you think he's honest?"

"I am talking about Shiamak Uncle's grandson," said Arjun, turning to his mother.

"Aah! Your school friend Mudit. He must be the best man for the job." Anjali smiled. Shiamak Trivedi had the reputation of having been the most honest and trustworthy director on the board of Mathur Industries. While Mudit and Arjun had been to the same school and had known each other for more than two decades.

Arjun nodded. "What are you writing nowadays?" he asked her. He was proud that his mother was a popular author of children's books and had four books and two series to her name, all published by a reputed international publisher.

"I'm working on a new series for twelve-year-olds."

"Awesome, Mom. I'm so proud of you."

"And do you know that Anjali has sold more than a million copies of her two dozen titles?" Parth said, getting up to refill his glass. "One more for you, Arjun?" He didn't bother to ask his wife as her capacity was only for one drink.

"Really!! Mom! When were you going to tell me? This calls for a celebration. Yes, Parth, I'll have another drink for sure. You must join us, Mom." He got up to pull her out of her sitting position and hugged her close. "You are a Rockstar!"

Anjali turned red, thrilled to hear her son's praise as she hugged him back. She beckoned to her husband and threw her other arm around him for a group hug, her cup of joy filled to overflowing.

It being a Friday, they chatted late into the night before Arjun got up to leave when he noticed his mother's valid attempts to cover her yawns. "I'll see you guys then. Thanks for the awesome drinks and meal, Parth."

"*Ho gaya?!* Just take yourself off, Brat. Give someone else your vote of thanks," grumbled Parth, bumping fists with his stepson as he saw him off.

Arjun felt the gripping pain in his heart ease a small bit as it always did after he spent some time with his mother and stepfather. But he knew for a fact that it will get right back to its original state when he woke up in the morning.

Life sucked! Horribly. He couldn't help wondering, as he had been doing for the past ten years, why he couldn't have died as well.

He was like a zombie, a walking-talking body without a soul.

iara Bakshi was excited to visit the Mathur Group of Industries' head office on Monday. She had an appointment with none other than the managing director, Arjun Mathur.

"Mr Mathur is ready to see you, Ms Bakshi." The receptionist called out to the waiting Kiara.

Kiara got up immediately to go to the bank of elevators. The managing director's office was based in the penthouse which was on the twenty-fifth floor. The lift carried her up swiftly before opening into yet another swanky reception hall.

"Ms Kiara Bakshi?" asked the man at the desk. When she nodded, he pointed her to a door on his left.

Kiara knocked on the door and entered when a voice invited her to, "Come in". Entering, Kiara blinked when bright sunlight hit her face, almost blinding her as she looked at the person sitting behind the huge office desk, working on his laptop. But she couldn't see beyond a vague outline. Presuming he must be the MD, she said, "Good morning, Mr Mathur."

"Please have a seat, Ms Bakshi. Mudit should be here soon. We'll start the meeting immediately after that." Arjun didn't look up at the woman who walked forward to sit in one of the visitors' chairs in front of his desk.

"Thanks," Kiara responded in a soft voice as she settled down in the chair. Blinking a couple of times, she got adjusted to the brightness before staring at the man behind the desk. He wore a dark blue suit teamed with a pristine white shirt and a silver-grey tie which had blood red motifs. His hair was brushed back neatly from his broad forehead, his eyebrows dark and thick. She couldn't see his eyes as he was engrossed in his work. But she couldn't miss the heavy eyelids and long, curling eyelashes any woman would die to have. A strong jawline, lean cheeks which were clean shaven and a square chin with a tiny cleft right in the middle made up the rest of the man's face. As for his lips— Kiara's gaze went wide as she ignored his thin upper lip when she noticed the sensual lower one. A man of infinite passion! She suppressed the giggle which rose in her throat, bringing her gaze down to her hands as they lay on her lap. For one with a chirpy nature, it was difficult to sit quiet and remain solemn.

But Mudit had warned her. He had told her how serious his boss was; that Arjun Mathur wouldn't tolerate her lively sense of humour. Indeed! Forget about his tolerance level, it looked like the man wasn't even aware that there was another person sitting right across his table.

"Coffee or tea?"

"Huh?" Kiara looked up, startled. "You said something?" Her mouth opened in a moue when she looked into his honey brown gaze and felt herself drowning in it. Oh my God! If his lips were drool worthy, his eyes were heart wrenching for want of a better expression.

"Ms Bakshi!" Arjun raised his voice to get her attention, a frown of irritation on his forehead. The woman was dumb or what?

"I'm sorry! You were saying?" Kiara reined in her racing thoughts to ask him.

"Will you have coffee or tea?"

"Coffee, please."

Mudit walked in after knocking, saying, "Sorry to keep you waiting, Arjun, Kiara."

Arjun waved him into the seat next to Kiara even as he lifted the phone to ask for three coffees.

"Hey, what's up?" Kiara gave Mudit a grin, her gamine face lighting up when she saw his friendly face. It was such a relief after staring at the MD's grim countenance over the last five minutes.

"All good. I'm glad you could make it despite your busy schedule, Kiara," said Mudit warmly.

"Shuddup! Don't be so damn formal." Kiara gave him a familiar pat on his forearm just as Arjun turned towards them.

"Arjun, this is Kiara Bakshi. I know you both have met, but let me give you some background. Kiara and I have been neighbours forever. And I can tell you she's the best hacker there is. She…

Arjun lifted a hand to stop Mudit mid-sentence. "This is the ethical hacker you spoke to me about?" She looked like a kid out of school. What the hell would she know about hacking? Arjun looked at her properly for the first time after she entered his cabin. With corkscrew curls which tumbled down her slender shoulders, her dark eyes dancing with mischief, her lips in a permanent pout, her pixie face was maybe the cutest he had ever set eyes on. But that was all the more reason for him to know that she was absolutely unsuitable for the work he needed done. "But… but she's a kid. I don't think she will do justice to…"

"Just a minute here." Kiara raised her left hand to stop Arjun mid-sentence even as she gripped Mudit's forearm with her right, not at all keen that he defend her. Facing the managing director of the Mathur Group of Industries head on, she continued, "I don't plan to tell you my age. But my credentials should speak for themselves." She turned to Mudit. "I sent you my bio. Haven't you shared it with your MD?" Again, before Mudit could reply, she said, "Okay, I see I have to prove myself here." She quickly took out her laptop and placing it on the table, booted it.

"Listen, Ms Bakshi, I don't have the time for this…"

"Five minutes. I just need five minutes of your time. You can throw me out after that." Kiara didn't look up at Arjun when she spat out the words, her focus on her laptop screen. Barely three minutes later, she smiled when Arjun's phone pinged. Looking him straight in the eye, she said, "I think you have mail."

With his frown growing deeper by the second, Arjun checked his phone. There was a mail saying that he had signed into his email using a new device.

Clenching his jaw, he glared at the grinning Kiara. "What does this mean?"

"I just hacked into your email account."

Arjun jumped up from his chair, snarling, "Get out. How can you bring her here, Mudit? You…"

Kiara lifted her hand, once again stopping Arjun mid-sentence. "You wanted to know if I am a good hacker and I just proved it. Shouldn't you be welcoming me with open arms instead of chucking me out of your office?"

Arjun spluttered, having a difficult time holding on to his temper. But he couldn't deny the logic in her words. Her black eyes danced even as her wide lips stretched even wider in a grin. Arjun bit his lip hard to stop the sudden smile which threatened to break out on his face. Yes, he had to agree she was good. But that didn't mean he was going to welcome her with a smile. With a tight look on his face, he admitted, "You're right, Ms Bakshi, welcome on board."

Kiara thrust her hand across the table, "Let's shake hands on that. And thanks, Arjun Mathur." She was impressed by the way he had admitted she was right.

Arjun, who had already turned to speak to Mudit, looked at her outstretched hand. Not having a choice, he took it in his to give it a shake, startled by the shot of electric current which passed from her hand to his. He quickly snatched his hand away and plopped down on his chair with a thud.

What the hell had happened just now?!

Arjun wasn't clear about the conversation flying around him over the next half an hour as Kiara and

Mudit discussed their plan of action. While he heard her voice and registered the multiple times her laughter rang out in his cabin, he couldn't grasp a word of what was being said.

When the meeting was over, Kiara got up from her chair, a grin on her face. "That was simply great. I think I will need a max of two weeks to crack this one. And yes, I can work from your office during that time."

Arjun stared at her, not really succeeding when he tried to keep the blank look out of his face as he got up from his chair too. Giving her a nod, he said, "That's fine, Ms Bakshi. When can you start?"

"Right now?" She lifted a shapely eyebrow as she looked into Arjun's eyes. *Was something bothering him? He appeared kind of dazed.*

"You can?" Arjun was surprised.

"That's great," said Mudit, clinching the matter. "I'll get HR to allot Kiara a cabin on the floor below. What say, Arjun?"

A small frown pleated Arjun's forehead. Mudit's office was on the twenty-fourth floor. And he didn't like the idea of Kiara Bakshi working there. Thinking quickly on his feet, he said, "Why not from the room next door, Mudit? The further Ms Bakshi is away from the accounts department, the better it is for us." That the accounts department was way down on the ninth floor and it really wouldn't make a difference whether Kiara was seated in the penthouse or one floor below was something neither man mentioned at that point.

"Perfect," said Mudit, giving his boss a smile and a nod. "Come along, Kiara. Let me show you to your office."

"Sure," said Kiara, linking her right hand to her friend's, even as she lifted her left hand in a wave to Arjun. "I'll see you around, then."

Arjun tilted his head in a small nod, his face unsmiling. No, he didn't like the familiarity between the newly appointed ethical hacker and his finance director, not one little bit.

nce Mudit left her on her own in the cabin, Kiara sat down in the swivel chair, staring at her laptop. There was a touch of red on her cheeks as her thoughts revolved around her meeting with Arjun Mathur.

The MD of the Mathur Group of Industries was not just handsome, but sizzling hot. She couldn't help feeling excited that she was going to work with him for two full weeks. Whoa!

She hadn't missed the electric spark when their hands connected during the brief shake. Would he have felt it as well? Kiara was somehow confident he had. A smile lit up her piquant face when she thought of the scene back there in his office. He had pulled his hand back so fast that it was indecent.

Arjun Mathur was extremely good-looking, yes. But something troubled him, deep down. Kiara hadn't missed the sadness at the back of his brown eyes. Eyes which were the colour of molten honey. Eyes she wanted to drown in.

Though the bitter experience with Harish had not made the bubbly Kiara cynical, it had made her wary of men. At seventeen, she had been enamoured by the stylish Harish, only to find out that he had been interested in her more because of her father's wealth than anything else. After that, she did her best to not fall for the ones who were after her money; or rather her father's money. What she never let on was how rich she personally was. While she had a legacy from her maternal grandparents, Kiara had made a lot of money from her profession as well. She was well-respected in her field, though she kept a low profile.

There had been a couple of boyfriends, and she had even slept with one of them. But neither had lasted long. Kiara had no issues being a single woman. In fact, she enjoyed the freedom of being single.

She opened her laptop to read the mail which Mudit had sent her. It contained the log in details to the office LAN. Mudit! Tall and dashing, he was the elder brother she had never had. It was a good thing that he treated her like a little sister as well. While they got along like a house on fire, they had never felt anything romantic for each other.

Kiara quickly logged into the LAN, running through the office floor plan meticulously. The Mathur offices were housed all over the twenty-five floors, with Arjun Mathur occupying the penthouse, with a man at the reception—Suraj Kanakia—and an executive assistant—Chintan Rao—in the cabin at his left. There were two more spacious cabins on the floor, to the right of the MD's, which had remained empty till now before Kiara was allotted one.

She recalled how Arjun had insisted she remain on this floor instead of moving down to the twenty-fourth where Mudit worked with his team. There were seven hundred and eighty-two people working in the building, all for the Mathur Group of Industries. In fact, the whole building—Indraprasth—belonged to the company. Besides this, they owned six factories all over North India.

Kiara was here to find out details of the state of the company's finances—what had been siphoned off during the last few years. That was what Arjun Mathur and Mudit suspected and they needed proof regarding the same.

Good! Catching crooks committing financial frauds was something Kiara was an expert at. It had all begun about a decade ago when her father had been swindled of five crore rupees…

Kiara Bakshi was seventeen years old when all hell broke loose, shattering the peaceful world she lived in. Her father Chandresh came home in the middle of the night, appearing torn to shreds.

"What happened, Chandresh?" asked an anxious Kalpana, Kiara's mother. She was used to her husband returning home latest by 8 pm every evening. That it was past midnight was a shock by itself.

"Everything's gone! All my earnings gone!" Chandresh buried his face in his hands, his body shaking with grief.

Young Kiara rushed to her father's side, placing a gentle hand on his shoulder. "Papa."

Kalpana sat on his other side. "Don't worry, Chandresh."

He lifted his tear-drenched face and looked at the two most important people in his life. "Someone hacked into my bank account and took out all our money." He gave a bitter laugh. "They were nice enough to leave two lakh rupees, to help us survive, I suppose."

"Whaaattt?????" Kalpana pressed both her hands to her cheeks, an expression of horror on her face. "They took away everything else?"

Kiara looked at her mother and father in turn. Even if she was only a teenager, she was well-versed with the family's finances. Her father, who had been born with a silver spoon, had improved his family's business, and had become a multimillionaire even before Kiara was born. Later, he had simply kept adding to their millions. While a large part of their wealth was in stocks and shares, Chandresh had kept a substantial amount in his bank as he needed the money for running his electronics business.

Had she understood him correctly? Had they been swindled for close to ten million rupees?

"Yes," said Chandresh, replying to his wife. "They have taken out five crore rupees in all."

Kiara paled. That was way more than what she had believed, closer to fifty million. How could that happen?

"Did you speak to the bank?" asked Kiara, holding her father's shoulder tightly, worried that his health might suffer because of this.

"Of course, I did," said Chandresh, turning to his daughter, trying to smile through his angst, but failing. "And I placed a complaint with the cyber cell the police directed me to."

"Is there a chance for the money to come back to us?" asked Kalpana, taking her husband's hand in hers.

Chandresh sighed. "There's a fifty-fifty chance, they say." He shrugged. "I don't really know."

"Papa, it's only money at the end of the day. We can always earn it back. Please don't be upset." Kiara spoke in a soft voice, pressing her cheek to his shoulder. Her father was her hero. And she didn't like him to be weak at any time.

Chandresh hugged his daughter close, another deep sigh shuddering through his body. "You are wise, my child; and absolutely right." He straightened his shoulders, continuing, "I won't be upset. After all, we still have a lot of wealth and beyond all that, I have you both." He threw his other arm around his wife and pulled her close.

"I hope the thief is arrested and convicted to lifetime imprisonment," said Kalpana in a rare show of temper. "How dare he take what is not his? You have worked so hard to earn that money."

Chandresh nodded, a smile breaking out on his face when he saw how angry his gentle wife was. "I have indeed. Let's see what the cyber cell does."

The Bakshis spent some quiet time at home, doing their best to digest the terrible crisis which had taken over their lives out of the blue.

It was much later when Kiara went to bed, checking her phone which had been lying in her bedroom, unattended. There were five missed calls from Harish.

She speed-dialled his number, not too worried that it was the middle of the night. He watched films late into the night, during the times he wasn't partying. "Hi Harish, sorry I couldn't take your call," she apologised the moment he answered.

"What was so important that you couldn't take my call?" Harish sounded angry.

Kiara sighed. "Something terrible, Harish. I didn't get a chance to go near my phone."

"Oh!" He sounded less angry when he asked, "What happened?"

They had been seeing each other over the last eight months and Kiara never kept anything from him. She quickly told him about the theft.

"Your father lost what?" Harish was screaming by now, unable to believe his ears.

"Close to fifty million rupees," said Kiara bluntly.

"But how dumb is that? How could your father be so careless?"

"Are you calling my father dumb?" While Kiara's voice was low, she was fuming by now. *How dare he accuse my father of being dumb?*

"Shouldn't he have done something to protect his money from thefts? Especially if he's going to have all of it lying in his bank account?"

All of it? Did Harish really believe that her father had lost all his wealth? Kiara turned a mite wary as she bit on a finger nail, a small scowl on her face.

She simply couldn't tolerate anyone saying anything demeaning about her father. "Listen Harish, my dad…"

"You listen, Kiara. You might worship your father and think he's the best man on earth. But I think he's a fool. He…"

Kiara disconnected the phone. It was a good thing Harish was not in front of her or she might have just slapped him. To hell with him! She didn't want a boyfriend in her life—not one who couldn't respect her father.

It had taken eight months of rigorous training before Kiara tracked down the thief who had stolen her father's money.

It hadn't been a single person but a whole syndicate. It had taken not only guts but great skill to bring down the whole bunch of fraudsters and hand them over to the cyber police. After that, Kiara had ensured the stolen money had been transferred back to her father's account, along with the interest he would have received from the bank. The top officers of the cyber cell were only too impressed with Kiara's work and had taken her help in many cases after that.

Till date, the syndicate had no clue what had hit them or who had caught them out. And Kiara had no plans of letting anyone trace it back to her. The first bit of training she had received was to cover her tracks and she had done just that.

With a smile, Kiara opened all confidential data belonging to the Mathur Group—the employee files, business transactions, accounts and more. She was in her element.

Bloody hell!

Arjun banged his clenched fists on his desk before jumping up from his chair. It was two hours after Mudit and Kiara left his office and he hadn't got any work done. Not one little bit!

He couldn't forget the sizzle he had felt when he touched Kiara's hand. He opened his right fist and held his hand up, staring at it as if to check if it contained burn marks. He could still feel her touch.

Why? Why now? Why her?

Arjun walked over to stand at the floor-to-ceiling window, his gaze unseeing as he stared down at the crisscross of private roads which connected the buildings in the Hiranandani Complex.

How was it even possible that this slip of a girl had got under his skin after all these years? The years he had spent away from women.

Too restless, Arjun paced his office, up and down, up and down. It had been a little more than a decade since Jane's death. It was also when he had found out she had betrayed him in such a terrible fashion. Arjun's heart had frozen during that time. It was as if he was in a state of penance. What Arjun didn't realise he was doing was that he was punishing himself for no fault of his.

The hurt, the pain, the anguish he had suffered at that time were something he never wanted to undergo ever again. It had been a twin blow. The life snuffed out of the love of his life in a flash while getting to know that she had never loved him. It had been as if someone had plunged a knife into his heart, only he hadn't been able to die and rest in peace. Jane had only loved his money and the luxurious life he could provide her.

At that time, Arjun had hated himself, believing that he wasn't worthy of being loved. While his best friend Krish and his stepfather Parth had managed to pull him out of his self-destructive attitude, they hadn't managed to retrieve Arjun from his state of apathy, an apathy he had slipped into, using it to cloak over his anger and hurt.

Deep down, Arjun was still the young man who had been deceived by the one woman he had trusted with all his heart. It was a little more than a decade but he still hadn't been able to let go of his hurt and anger.

4

About a decade back…

Jane Mckenzie was busy at the takeaway counter serving a customer when her mobile buzzed. She ignored it as she placed the chicken burger, French fries, and chocolate milkshake on a tray before adding some tissues to it, smiling at the customer as she handed it over to him.

A small scowl formed on her neat forehead when her phone buzzed again. Every one of her friends and acquaintances knew that she worked in the evenings. Who the hell was calling her again and again?

"Could you please takeover for a couple of minutes? The call seems urgent." Jane requested Bill who was serving right next to her.

"Get back ASAP," said Bill, frazzled. After all, the counter was at its busiest at that time of the evening.

"Sure," she said before walking through the back door. Seeing Arjun's face on her phone, she took the call, saying, "What's the rush, Arjun?"

"Something has happened," replied Arjun in a choked voice. "Listen, Jane. I have to go home. There's an emergency…"

"Again?" Jane bit back her sigh of exasperation. Arjun Mathur and his family! Tch! He came with a lot of baggage, it seemed. And she had believed life would be such fun with him—Arjun being loaded with money and all that. But this constant need to keep visiting his family back in India was rather wearing on her nerves. "What's wrong now?"

It was only a few months back when his mother had been sick, suffering from depression is what he had told her. It looked like Indian parents were very different from British ones. They were too damn dependent on their grownup children.

"Jane, my father's dead. He was murdered… I…"

"What?" *Is he having me on*? "Are you serious?" she asked him outright.

Arjun gave a bitter laugh, biting back a sob. "You really don't believe I'd joke about something like this."

She supposed not! "What happened?" she asked impatiently. Bill was waiting for her to return to her post and he was capable of complaining to the management if she didn't go back in a couple of minutes.

"I'm not sure, except that he was shot in his bed."

"I'm sorry to hear about it, Arjun." Well, Arjun had been close to his father and must be feeling sad, maybe even devastated. But Jane was simply not interested. It looked like her relationship with him was definitely not worth all this emotional baggage, even if he came with a lot of money. "You must be in a hurry anyway. You get home and give me a call. I *need* to rush back… I'm sure you understand."

"Of course, Jane. I'm at the airport actually. Just wanted to say bye."

"Bye. And you take care," she added as an afterthought, her heart jumping to her throat in excitement. She was going to have the swanky apartment all to herself. Woohoo!

Completely unaware that his live-in girlfriend loved his money rather than himself, Arjun caught his flight from London's Heathrow airport to Mumbai, keeping his tears at bay with great difficulty. Jayant Mathur had been murdered in bed. He simply couldn't believe that his larger-than-life father was no more.

It was past eleven o'clock when Peter Frazer rang the bell to Arjun's apartment. He rubbed his hands in glee, a wide smile on his face as he waited for Jane to open the door. Wasn't it a good thing that Arjun had gone away to India? Jane wasn't even sure when he was coming back.

"Hey, come on in," invited Jane, a big smile on her face as she took his hand and pulled him inside.

Peter gathered her in his arms and kissed her hard, desperate for her as she wouldn't let him lay a hand on her when Arjun was around. Which seemed to be all the time.

"I want you, Babe. And don't you dare say no," Peter growled, his face buried in the crook of her shoulder.

Jane gave a husky laugh, her arms around his trim waist. "You can have all of me, you idiot. Arjun won't be returning anytime soon. This place is like a palace." Neither Peter nor Jane was born into riches and had to work hard to get through university.

Peter loved Jane from the depth of his heart. A year senior to both Jane and Arjun, he had given up on her when she had entered into a live-in relationship with Arjun.

It was six months ago when Jane had kept him on tenterhooks with her smouldering come-hither looks and gentle touches. That was the time when Arjun had left her alone at his apartment to go to India — something about his mother being sick. Anyway, it didn't really matter to Peter. He was only interested in Jane.

Even now, he didn't like the idea of her living with Arjun. But Jane was clear about what she wanted from life. "Come on, Peter. This apartment is damn luxurious compared to the hostel room and I can even save the rent. And the poor sod really believes I love him."

"But you must have some feelings for him, right?" Peter had asked, jealousy tearing at his innards.

Jane had given him a wicked smile. "Will I be making love to you like this if I am in love with him?"

Peter was too much in love with her to care; and was ready to accept whatever crumbs which came his way. While he didn't like Jane two-timing Arjun, he accepted that she enjoyed the life of luxury as Arjun's girlfriend.

"I don't like it though," he declared now, "you being with Arjun when it's me you love."

"It won't be for long." Peter wasn't to know that Jane had stored away every bit of jewellery and cash Arjun had showered her with. She had even collected all the other gifts he had given her, planning to keep what she really liked and sell everything else. She was going to make a lot of money that way. "Why don't we stop discussing Arjun and make love?" she asked in a sexy purr, making Peter melt.

Peter forgot his own name, let alone Arjun's when they fell into bed with each other.

P arth was in a fuming temper when he caught the Emirates flight from Mumbai non-stop to London, after Arjun's desperate call.

"Parth, please come over." The twenty-year-old Arjun had pleaded tearfully, barely a few hours back.

"Is everything alright?" asked Parth, concern in his voice.

"No!" Arjun's voice was an angry growl. "My whole life's in shambles. Jane died in an accident. And Parth… I…" His voice petered away into silence before he completed the sentence.

"Oh my God! I'm terribly sorry, Arjun." Parth shut his eyes in horror. Jane had been so young, barely nineteen. "I'm coming right away. Let me talk to your mother…"

"Don't, Parth. Don't tell Mom anything." Arjun's voice cracked, grounding to a stop once again as he was unable to go on.

"Are you sure?" Anjali was bound to be hurt if no one told her about Jane.

Arjun sniffed. "That's not the whole of it, Parth. I… I'm in the hospital…"

"Were you also in the accident, Arjun?" Parth jumped up from his chair, walking agitatedly around the apartment, shaken more than before. He adored his stepson and thought of Arjun as his own child. "How badly are you hurt?"

"No, I wasn't in the accident that took Jane away from me."

"I don't understand. Then why are you in the hospital?" Parth stopped in his tracks to ask, a deep scowl on his face.

"I cut my wrist, Parth." Arjun's voice was a whisper before it rose in anger, "I don't want to live anymore," he shouted. "Not now that my Jane is gone. But… I survived, Parth. I didn't bleed long enough. They have admitted me in the hospital and here I am." His voice had become weak once again and it was obvious that he was crying.

It was with a tremendous effort that Parth held back his temper. Arjun had attempted to commit suicide! Anjali's son; the brave young man who had been a pillar of rock at the time of his father's death by murder. The one who had forgiven Jayant Mathur's murderer without too much effort. The mature boy who had befriended Parth at Café Coffee Day and had encouraged his mother to lead an independent life!

How the hell could that same Arjun want to take his own life?

That Parth was flummoxed was putting it mildly. He immediately booked a one-way ticket to London, not clear about how long he might have to stay there; only for himself. No way was he going to tell Anjali about what her son had done. Time enough when he returned to Mumbai after setting things straight.

"Hey sweetheart!" Parth hugged Anjali when she let herself into the apartment at five in the evening. She had been out with a friend for lunch and a movie.

"Parth!" Anjali snuggled closer to her husband of less than a year, kissing him fully on his lips. "Miss me?"

"Every second you aren't with me," he responded, giving her an adoring smile. "But listen, I need to rush to London. I'm…"

"Huh? When? Let me go pack…"

"I already have. I'm going by the midnight Emirates flight. I…"

She frowned up at him. "Why am I not going with you?"

Parth lifted a hand to gently run it over her forehead, wiping the frown off her face. "My agent has set up a meeting with a publisher and wants me there like yesterday." It didn't matter that he was lying through his teeth to his wife with whom he shared an honest relationship. Right now, the situation warranted it. "And you have your book reading session the day after tomorrow. It doesn't make sense cancelling it."

Anjali wrinkled her nose at him. "I forgot all about it. But I'm going to miss you, Parth. How long do you plan to be away?"

"I haven't booked my return as yet. Let me find out more when I get there. If I need to be there for long, you can always join me. What say?"

"I say yes." Anjali gave him a wide smile.

It was a wonder that the sensitive Anjali didn't notice the flaming temper her husband was in, having difficulty keeping it under wraps. For the first time in his life, Parth was so damn angry with his stepson.

How dare he! How dare Arjun attempt to take his own life!

Parth couldn't concentrate on anything during the nine-and-a-half-hour flight; not on his writing nor on his reading. He ran through the list of films on offer during the flight and found none of them interesting. His mind kept returning to Arjun.

Arjun had been barely nineteen when they first met at the coffee shop in Hiranandani Gardens, Powai, where they both lived. Parth had found the young man familiar before he got to know that Arjun was Anjali Mathur's—at that time, Anjali was married to Jayant Mathur, Arjun's father—son.

Parth and Arjun had got along like a house on fire from the moment they met. Arjun had been feeling low because his mother had been suffering from depression and had found it easy to talk about it to a stranger.

That was the beginning of a beautiful relationship between Parth and his now stepson, Arjun. It was Arjun who had been in full support when Parth showed a romantic interest in Anjali and had gone on to marry her later.

Parth had been a steady support to Anjali and Arjun at the time of Jayant's murder and later when they had hired a private detective to trace the murderer. Arjun, still a teenager at that time, had shown tremendous maturity when he forgave his father's murderer, who had got away with only three years' jail term, all thanks to Arjun's efforts.

How could that same Arjun attempt suicide? Parth could believe it only because it had been Arjun himself who had given him the news.

Shit! Why was life such a bitch?

njali rubbed a gentle forefinger over the silky head of Sam, her pet cat who was purring in pleasure, her mind turning inward.

Had Parth seemed disturbed about something? Just now she recalled that he hadn't been himself. Usually chatty, he hadn't said much and hadn't even shown an appetite for dinner; one who always enjoyed his food.

Considering that he was going to be away from her for at least a week, Parth hadn't shown any interest in making love to her. And that had been the bigger surprise. Anjali never hesitated to invite him to bed, not being shy around him at all. But somehow, his body language hadn't encouraged it. Sensitive to his moods, she had accepted the absent-minded peck on her cheek before he took off.

They had sex almost every night and sometimes even in the day. Anjali sat up straight. It struck her that something must be seriously wrong. Looking at the wall clock in the sitting room, she realised that Parth must have crossed security and must be waiting to board his flight. Taking her phone, she speed-dialled his number.

"Parth!"

"Hi sweetheart, you must be sleepy." He needed to be careful of what he spoke to her.

"Yeah, a bit. But tell me, what's wrong?"

"Wrong?" Parth didn't really laugh it off as she had expected him to. "Of course, nothing's wrong. Why do you ask?"

"Are you hiding something from me?" Anjali asked outright. Not that she expected her husband to cheat on her. Parth simply wasn't wired that way, not at all. He was as honest as they came.

He laughed. "Are you crazy? What will I want to hide from you?"

Anjali noticed the strain in his laughter. Not keen to bother him more than he already was, she said, "That's true. I must have imagined it. You take care and have a safe flight. Do give my love to Arjun when you meet him." A trip to London wasn't complete without meeting Arjun as he was studying at the Kingston University and she knew how close the two men in her life were, even though they weren't related by blood.

"I'll do that. And Anjali, sweetheart, you do know that I love you with all my heart, don't you?"

Anjali was thrilled to hear the words he whispered so passionately. With a wide smile, she replied, "Oh yes, Parth! I do. Tell me again though."

"I love you, my Anjali, from the bottom of my heart," said Parth in a voice gone rough with passion.

"And I love you, my Parth. You are the best thing that happened to me after Arjun," said Anjali, equally passionately. "You take care and come back soon." She blew him a kiss, adoring her second husband. It was barely a few hours since he left home but she was already missing him badly.

Arjun opened his eyes a slit to see who it was who had entered his room in the private hospital in Central London, not really surprised when he realised it was Parth.

"Hello, Parth!"

"How dare you?" Parth's voice was a muted roar as he glared at his stepson.

Arjun turned pale on hearing Parth's words. They were friends first and had become related later when Arjun's mother Anjali got married to Parth Bhardwaj. And Arjun had been all for the match as he had only wanted his mother's happiness. Unable to lift a hand in greeting—his left wrist heavily bandaged while an IV tube was connected to his other hand—Arjun gave the older man a small nod.

"Tell me, Arjun! How dare you try to kill yourself?" Parth was ready to blow his top. With an effort at calming down, he plopped himself on the chair next to Arjun's bed.

Arjun was completely stunned. Parth, so even tempered, with a well of patience—how come he was so angry? Especially in Arjun's hour of need? When he was suffering from such a terrible loss too. Shouldn't he be supportive instead?

Arjun couldn't stop the tears which ran down the sides of his face, soaking his pillow wet. "Parth…"

Parth shook his head at Arjun. "I never thought you were a coward; not Anjali's son. How the hell could you…?"

"Parth," Arjun protested weakly, "why are you so angry, Parth?" he asked, deeply hurt.

Parth jumped up from the chair he was sitting on and walked around the room a couple of times, his hands clenched into tight fists. He stopped next to Arjun and held the younger man's face in both his hands. "How could you, Arjun?"

"I don't want to live, Parth. Not after the accident which took Jane away from me," said Arjun in a broken voice, a pathetic expression on his face.

"So, how long have you known Jane? Two years? Or less?" Parth was relentless in his questioning.

"Nineteen months. Jane was my life. She…"

"Seriously! What would she think of you if she saw you just now? You think she'd want to be in a relationship with a coward?" Parth was deliberately cruel as he pinned Arjun with his sharp silver gaze.

The little blood which was there drained out of Arjun's face. "How dare you, Parth? *How dare you*? Can't you see it from my point of view? Can't you see how heartbroken I am? Can't you…?"

"Nothing in the world gives you the right to break your mother's heart." Parth said firmly. "Anjali has suffered too much pain in her life. It has been less than a year since she has found some happiness. How do you think she'd have faced your death? That too by suicide?" Parth drove the point home, standing tall next to Arjun's bed, clenched fists on his hips as he glared down at his stepson, a deep scowl on his face.

"Parth!" It was a howl of torment as Arjun stared up at his best friend's accusing face, begging for understanding.

The anger left Parth in a whoosh as he leaned down to place a pacifying hand on the younger man's head. "Oh Arjun! What will I do with you?"

"Jane is gone, Parth," cried Arjun, his voice breaking, "she was charred to death when the car blew up in flames. She's no more, Parth…"

Parth brushed back the hair which had fallen on Arjun's forehead, drying his tears with tissues from a box on the side table, not saying anything, allowing Arjun to continue.

"…and you know what?" Arjun hiccupped, making an effort to stop crying.

"Tell me," invited Parth in a soothing voice, his anger having disappeared completely.

"She was eloping with Peter, our senior from college, when his car crashed." Arjun turned the other way, trying to bury his hurt along with his face in the hospital pillow. That had been worse than her death, completely below the belt.

Arjun had been sure that Jane loved him. They had been so happy in the apartment he had bought for them in London. And how she had protested about not being able to contribute to the expenses! He had shushed her, every time. And all along, she had been two-timing him.

Arjun felt as if his heart would explode with the pain and betrayal.

"How do you know they were eloping? They could have been…"

Arjun turned around in a flash, his eyes dry now but red-rimmed with temper. "She was in the driver's seat when the car crashed. Peter hadn't been wearing the seat belt and was thrown clear. He lived to tell the tale."

It had been a terrible moment when Arjun had rushed to the hospital to see Peter who had got away with minor scratches. "Why was Jane driving your car?" Arjun had hollered at the other man, his voice demented.

"She insisted, bro." Peter's face was streaked with dirt and dried up tear tracks.

"Why would Jane insist on driving your car? She could have driven mine anytime." She had always refused, insisting that she didn't want to scratch Arjun's expensive BMW.

"You really didn't know her, did you?" Peter gave Arjun a pitying look.

"Shuddup, you bastard. I knew Jane better than anyone else in our campus." Arjun didn't care it was the hospital as he shouted louder than ever, unable to bear the crushing pain in his heart. Jane was dead! And this bastard was responsible for it.

Peter shook his head. "You didn't, Arjun. Or you'd have known what we were up to," he said in a broken voice.

"What?" Arjun scowled at the other man. What was he getting at?

"We were on our way to get married, in secret."

Arjun punched Peter on his nose, feeling a sense of satisfaction when he heard the crunch of bone breaking, turning right around to run out of the hospital.

Jane had been two-timing me! For how long?

In a fit of madness, Arjun reached his apartment, took his razor, and slit his left wrist, watching the blood ooze out in morbid fascination. Yes, life wasn't worth living, not after loving and losing Jane. And as for the betrayal, he didn't want to face life, not any more.

Krish Sanyal, also a student at Kingston University, rang Arjun's doorbell. He got to know about Jane's accident and had also found out about her attempted elopement with Peter.

Krish felt upset for his best friend's sake. Arjun and Krish used to hang out together a lot before Jane came into the former's life. After that she had taken up most of Arjun's time and Krish had been happy for them.

And all this while she had been two-timing Arjun! No one seemed to know for how long. Krish had seen Arjun breaking Peter's nose at the hospital but instead of rushing behind his friend, he had stopped to help Peter, calling a nurse to his aid.

Overcome by pain and anguish, Peter had shouted, "Jane never loved him. It was me she loved."

"Then why didn't she simply tell him so?" Krish had asked, his soft voice a complete contrast to the other man's loudness.

"Arjun never let her. He smothered her with his wealth. The idiot had a different name for it though. He called it love." Peter's voice was utterly sarcastic.

Krish's eyes went wide in surprise. "Do you even know what you are talking about? You bastard! If Arjun hadn't already broken your nose, it would have been an absolute pleasure to do it for him."

Making an about turn, Krish walked out of the hospital ward, got into his car to follow Arjun to his home. He was sure that that was where his friend must have gone to lick his wounds in private.

Krish could see that the light was on inside, but no one came to open the door. He waited for a few minutes, a frown on his face. Maybe Arjun was in the bathroom. When the door didn't open even after five minutes, Krish opened the lock with the spare key he had and pushed it open. "Arjun?"

Hearing someone crying bitterly, he followed the sound to the bedroom and rushed inside to find Arjun on the floor, his wrist bleeding. "What the fuck…! You idiot! Arjun!"

Krish jumped forward to take Arjun's left hand in his and saw his life blood trickling away. Arjun was as pale as a ghost even as he whimpered, tears streaming down his face.

Krish quickly opened the wardrobe and took out a handkerchief from a drawer before tying it tightly in the middle of Arjun's forearm, doing his best to stop the bleeding. While it reduced, it didn't stop completely.

With an arm around Arjun's shoulders, Krish pulled his friend up to his feet and made him stand. "Can you walk?"

"Leave me alone, Krish. I wanna die."

Krish ignored his words, asking him again, "Can you walk?"

"Let me go," Arjun's voice was a tormented growl.

"No way. I'm taking you to the hospital. And remember to thank me for it in maybe a year or two."

Krish dragged Arjun out of the apartment as he half carried him down the single flight of stairs, all the way to his car. Pulling the passenger door open, Krish pushed Arjun inside before shutting the door firmly, glad that the latter was too weak to protest by now. Jogging to the other side, he got into the driver's seat and drove away as if the devil was chasing him.

It was lucky that all traffic lights were green before Krish stopped his car in front of the private hospital's lobby. Soon, Arjun was wheeled away on a stretcher.

Luckily, Arjun hadn't bled too much and didn't require blood transfusion, though the case needed to be reported to the police and there was a lot of paperwork.

Krish insisted that Arjun should call his home.

"I don't want to talk to my mom." Arjun had protested, glaring at his best friend.

"I will call her if you don't," threatened Krish right back. While he could sympathise with his friend's actions, he still felt that Arjun's mother needed to know.

"You wouldn't!" Arjun protested.

"Try me."

"But Krish, Mom will be heartbroken. She has only recently found happiness after a miserable twenty years."

"And you realise that now, you idiot! What do you think would have happened to her if you had killed yourself?"

Arjun turned paler than he already was, his eyes darkening with pain as he turned his face away towards the wall.

"So, will you call your mother? Or should I?" Krish was relentless.

"Let me call Parth, my stepfather."

Krish breathed a sigh of relief. "Do that." He waited till he heard Arjun speaking to Parth Bhardwaj before leaving him in peace.

Once he got to know that Arjun's stepfather was on his way to London, Krish said, "I am taking myself off now. Will catch you tomorrow morning. You take care, okay? And get well soon."

"Krish…" Arjun's voice was a cry of anguish. "I miss her, Krish. My Jane is no more."

"Jane was never yours in the first place," said Krish brutally, his body going rigid with anger as he thought of her betrayal. "The bitch never loved you. Don't forget that, ever."

Krish held Arjun's hand for a pacifying moment before leaving him alone. He went to meet the nurse in charge of Arjun's room and requested her to keep an eye on the patient. What if he tried to kill himself again?

9

After being discharged from hospital, Arjun had continued to be angry with Parth for a few days, not even speaking to him properly.

Anjali arrived a few days after Arjun was back home. Between the two of them, Parth and Arjun had kept the latter's suicide attempt from her. That was one thing both men were completely in agreement about. Anjali should not be upset unnecessarily.

Consequently, Jane's betrayal was also not mentioned. Anjali had presumed that Arjun was terribly upset about Jane's death. As a result, both Parth and Anjali had spent a few more weeks in London at Arjun's apartment.

It wasn't easy, but it wasn't long before Arjun's sense of rightness was restored and he could see the whole scenario from Parth's view point.

It was early one morning as the two of them were out jogging when Arjun stopped in his tracks, his hand on Parth's arm. "Please forgive me, Parth. You were absolutely right. I shouldn't have tried to kill myself. My Mom definitely doesn't deserve more pain."

Parth hugged the younger man. "There's nothing to forgive, Brat. And it's not just about Anjali. You, my dear Arjun, *you* don't deserve to die at such a young age. You have so much. And you can do so much. And at the end of the day, son, Jane wasn't worthy of either your love or your loyalty, was she? She definitely didn't deserve such a big sacrifice from you. Taking your life for her sake wouldn't have been worth it."

Arjun sighed, biting his lip to stop the tears which peeped out of his eyes. "It was a moment of madness," he agreed, though his voice was bitter. Suddenly, it rose to a high pitch when he yelled, "I know you're right. But that still doesn't stop me from missing her, Parth."

Parth placed a firm hand on Arjun's shoulder. "Please be aware that you are in love with your image of Jane, not the real person. The Jane of your imagination simply does not exist. She never did. Do you understand?"

Arjun turned angry eyes to Parth, glaring into his silver gaze, wanting to punch him.

But Parth refused to budge, meeting the younger man's gaze head on, willing him to see sense and calm down.

"Aaarrrgh!" Arjun bent double before going on his haunches, screaming at the top of his voice, his fists banging on his thighs. "I hate myself," he yelled.

Parth crossed his arms across his chest and let Arjun howl to his heart's content, waiting patiently for the storm to blow over.

It was a long time before Arjun got up to stand straight, his head lowered as he couldn't look the other man in the eye.

Parth placed a hand under Arjun's chin and lifted his face. "Do you feel better?"

Arjun took a deep breath, then another one before a glimmer of a smile broke out on his face. "Actually, I do."

"I don't know how you feel about yourself, but believe me when I say that I love you." Parth reached out to kiss his stepson on his forehead. "And I don't have to tell you about what your mother thinks of you."

"I'm lucky to have two people who love me so much," said Arjun, his voice hoarse with emotion.

"Want to get a proper English breakfast? I'm famished after all that emotional drama." Parth lifted an eyebrow at Arjun.

Arjun nodded. "Sure, why not? I think my body can do with some refuelling as well."

Yes, he was better. And yes, he didn't want to kill himself or hate himself any longer. But Arjun was clear he wanted nothing to do with women, not ever.

Women were selfish! They took men for granted and didn't care for their feelings. For them, it was all about how much to get out of any relationship. Jane had not only betrayed Arjun, she had also treated Peter in a shabby way. While she had used Arjun for his wealth, she had expected Peter to stand by and do nothing about the affair she was having with Arjun. How terrible was that!

During the time at home while recovering from his failed suicide attempt and his girlfriend's death, Arjun had had a lot of time to think. To begin with, he realised that killing himself was not the solution. Parth had been right. His mother had found happiness after such a long time. It wouldn't be fair for her to lose her only son, the son whom she adored.

But while Arjun had realised that suicide wasn't the solution, he had changed overnight for the worse. The compassionate and adorable young man had become a cynical woman-hater.

Left to his devices, there wouldn't be a single woman working in his office and company. But unable to give up his sense of fairness, he hadn't ousted the women—three hundred and ninety-seven of them—who already worked for his company. But the new recruits were generally from the male sex, at least those employees who needed to be vetted by the MD himself.

Arjun slowly came back to the present as he had been lost down memory lane.

Ten years! Arjun had lived the life of penance for ten years, staying completely away from women. He had placed his heart on deep freeze mode and refused to let it thaw. And to be fair, there had been no reason for it to soften up. He had simply refused to interact with women.

There were people who sniggered behind his back, calling him a Buddha. Arjun was even aware of it. Not that he cared.

It was with great difficulty he had achieved this state of calm, wrapping himself in a cocoon which kept women at bay. He didn't want to depend on the female species for anything. The only woman he trusted was his mother. Wasn't it a good thing he wasn't dependent on her for anything? And Anjali would never demand anything from her son, at least nothing he wouldn't want to give her.

But today, it looked like his very foundation, the comfort zone which he had settled into for over a decade, was shaken.

Kiara!

The young lady who had walked into his office today had been like a breath of fresh air. In one visit, she had somehow managed to tear through the cobwebs of his past and reached to his inner core. So much so that Arjun felt threatened.

All it had taken was the soft touch of her feminine hand!

"Hello, Smita Aunty!" Arjun took the call to greet his father's younger sister.

"Arjun *Beta*! How are you?" Smita asked fondly. She had adored her brother Jayant from the day he was born. After Jayant's death, she had transferred all that love to his son.

"I'm good, Aunty. So, tell me. How are you? And Rana Uncle?"

"We are all fine, Arjun. I wanted to share some wonderful news with you. Ritu is getting married next week. I have already posted the wedding invitation to you. It's on January 19, at the Hyatt Regency. The *muhurat* is at 9.30 am. You should join us for breakfast and lunch. Then there is the reception from 7 to 11 pm. I don't have to tell you how much I miss your father…" Her voice had dwindled to a choked whisper by now.

"I'll definitely be there, Aunty. Have you sent an invite to Mom and Parth?" Arjun had a gut feeling about this.

Smita cleared her throat a little too loudly. There was a pause as if she was searching for the right words before speaking, "Listen, Arjun. You are my blood and…"

"…and my Mom isn't. But Aunty, you're forgetting that I'm not only your brother's son but also my mother's. You listen carefully! I'll attend the wedding only if you invite my mother and stepfather. Otherwise, let me wish you all the best. I'll mail you a cheque to cover the wedding expenses." After all, isn't it what she was expecting from him? If his father had been alive, they would have fleeced Jayant for a lot more than that.

Smita began to cry loudly. "How can you talk like this, Arjun? You know how much Rana Uncle and I love you. And you also know very well that your mother has no…"

"STOP RIGHT THERE! With all due respect to you and Rana Uncle, I will not tolerate one word of abuse against my mother. Do you hear, Smita Aunty? If you say anything at all about her, you might as well forget the cheque."

He disconnected the call, not bothering to wait for her response.

It was an hour later when Anjali called her son. "Arjun!"

"Hey Mom."

"Are you trying to buy me some respect with your money, by any chance?" Anjali sounded furious.

"Huh?! What's this about?"

"Did you threaten Smita about not giving her a cheque if she doesn't invite me and Parth to Ritu's wedding?"

"Come again!"

"You heard me."

"Do you want to hear my side or have you already judged me?" Arjun couldn't help smiling as he wasn't really surprised by his mother's reaction.

"Idiot! Tell me."

"I told Smita Aunty that I would courier the cheque to her if she had no plans to invite you and Parth. Was I wrong?"

"Why do you want to force us down your father's relatives' throats?" Anjali was vexed.

"Well, I agree that I'm related to them. But my primary relationship is with you and Parth. They can't treat you with disrespect and want to be friends with me." Arjun was too clear about that.

"Fair enough. But what do you plan to achieve by insisting that we be present at this wedding, Arjun?"

"Mom! Don't you love Ritu?"

"Of course, I do." Anjali genuinely loved her husband's niece and the feelings were reciprocated with equal enthusiasm. "And I have invited Ritu and her husband home for dinner after they return from their honeymoon."

"But don't you want to attend her wedding?"

"Does it matter? You very well know why. Her parents don't want me there." Especially Rana. Ritu's father hated his brother-in-law's wife and had made his feelings obvious right from the beginning. The hatred had only increased manifold when Anjali had married Parth.

"Ritu does. I hope that counts."

"Aww! Did she say so?"

"Yes. Which is why I asked Smita Aunty to invite you and Parth. And I didn't threaten her about the cheque, at least not in the way she put it across to you. Listen, Mom. I'm not going to sit back and listen to her heaping abuse on your head, okay? I..."

"Okay, okay. I get the picture. By the way, your aunt, shedding copious tears, invited me to the wedding. Even Parth."

"Good! Would you like me to pick up both of you on Sunday morning? By eight?"

"Do I have a choice?" Anjali sounded miffed.

"Come on, Mom. For Ritu's sake?"

"I suppose."

"They did invite Parth too, right?"

"Of course, they did, Arjun. The power of money and all that, you know."

Arjun's answering laugh was sarcastic. "Don't I!"

They chatted for a few minutes more before Anjali rang off.

Checking the silver watch on his left wrist, Arjun got up from his chair. It was past two. He might as well get some lunch at the canteen. He wasn't getting any work done anyway.

Mudit and Kiara were chatting nineteen to a dozen as they munched their way through the subsidised lunch at the office canteen when Arjun walked in. If Mudit was surprised to see his boss in the canteen, he didn't show it. After all, Arjun was the most unpredictable person he knew.

They had known each other from school days as Mudit's grandfather had been associated with Jayant Mathur's company from its nascency. Of course, Arjun had been a different person during those days.

"Hey Arjun! Want to join us?" Mudit called out.

"Why not?" While he spoke to Mudit, Arjun's eyes were on Kiara's animated face, an acrid attack of jealousy attacking his insides as he couldn't help but notice her closeness to Mudit. "Let me get something to eat. Do you guys want anything?"

"Not me," said Mudit, turning his head towards Kiara.

"I'd like some coffee, please."

Arjun gave a nod as he walked to the service counter.

The chef walked out of the kitchen when he got to know that the MD was in the canteen on one of his rare visits. "Good afternoon, sir. What can I get you? Today's special is *aloo gobhi* and *paneer makhani*. There's also *butter roti* to go with it."

Arjun shook his head. "I heard there was *mattar paratha* for breakfast. Will it be possible to have a couple of those with a bowl of *mixed veggie raita*?" His front office man, Suraj Kanakia, had been all praise for it.

"But, of course, sir. I'll personally make it all fresh in ten minutes. I hope you don't mind the wait."

"That will be alright, Nandlal. May I have two cups of coffee for now?"

One of the assistants, Vikas, rushed forward with two cups of coffee after he caught the head chef's eye. "I'll bring it over to your table, sir."

"Give it to me, Vikas," said Arjun firmly, not leaving the man with a choice. Taking the tray, he walked over to the table where Mudit and Kiara were seated. "Here you go," he said, offering one cup to Kiara before taking his.

"Thank you," said Kiara with a brilliant smile. "Aren't you eating anything?"

"They are making fresh *parathas* for me." Arjun sipped from his cup, unable to move his gaze away from her.

"Ooh! They are! I wish I had known. I'd have preferred to have *parathas* too. What is the filling?"

Arjun gave her one of his rare smiles. "Peas. Should I ask them to make some for you as well?" He turned around to lift a finger in the direction of the counter, only to be stopped by Kiara's hand on his arm. He couldn't stop the sudden hot flush which rose up from the core of his body all the way up to his face. "What is it?" he asked her, his voice hoarse.

"Not for me. I'm full." She patted her flat stomach, inadvertently drawing his gaze to her slender figure.

With tremendous effort, Arjun drew his gaze away from her to focus on Mudit. "So, what's up, Mudit? Will you be at Ritu's wedding?"

"Yeah. Ritu sent me the invite on WhatsApp." Mudit turned to Kiara and explained, "Ritu is Arjun's cousin. We all went to the same school."

Kiara gave a nod, continuing to drink her coffee, her eyes half shut as she surreptitiously studied Arjun's face. She hadn't missed the colour on his face when she placed a hand on his arm. Was he as aware of her as she was of him? She sat quietly, listening to the two of them talk.

Mudit was surprised to see the bubbly Kiara go silent, but refrained from commenting.

Head Chef Nandlal Baradia himself brought a tray with a plate of steaming hot parathas with butter melting over them, along with a bowl of *raita*. "Here you go, sir. I hope you like it."

"I'm sure I will, Nandlal. Thank you," said Arjun, taking a deep whiff of the aroma wafting from the freshly made food. "Have a bite," he invited Kiara.

I'd rather have a bite of you! Kiara couldn't help the thought which sprang to her mind on hearing his words. Without saying anything, she broke a piece of paratha with her hand and popped it into her mouth, her eyes closing as she munched on it. It simply melted in her mouth.

Watching the sensual play of rapture on her face, Arjun asked, "Changed your mind?"

Kiara opened her eyes to gaze into his honey brown ones, giving a small shake of her head. "I agree it's amazing. But I just had a lunch plate, the whole works."

Mudit got up from his chair. "I have a call in five. You'll both have to excuse me." He was sure that neither of them was even aware when he left.

"How come you landed up learning ethical hacking?" Arjun asked Kiara.

"I was seventeen when someone hacked into my father's bank account and wiped it almost clean." There was no anger in Kiara's voice when she spoke about the incident which had transformed her life. "Though it wasn't the whole lot of our wealth, it ran into millions. I was lucky to be able to change my mind and train in ethical hacking instead of becoming a computer engineer."

Arjun stopped eating as he stared at her in fascination. "You changed your mind, just like that?"

Kiara nodded, the curls bouncing all around her face. "The very next morning, I searched on the internet and found a lot of information about ethical hacking. In the beginning, my father wasn't too keen. He was worried I might land in trouble if I went after criminals." She laughed, the tinkling sound music to Arjun's ears. "But in the end, he accepted. He was the first one to admit that I have my head firmly screwed to my shoulders." She grinned at Arjun.

"So, how many years of experience do you have in this hacking line?"

"If you want to know my age, why don't you ask me straight?" Kiara winked at him.

Arjun burst out laughing, surprising himself. It took a while for his mirth to subside before he said, "I know you'll be twenty-seven come September." He winked right back at her.

He must have read her CV!

Her eyes danced when she looked into his glowing brown gaze. "And how old are you? I think it's only fair since you know my age."

"I turned thirty some months back."

"Hmm." She placed her empty coffee cup on the table, watching him eat. It took no effort and gave her infinite pleasure. He was probably the handsomest man she had ever set eyes on. Mudit had warned her that Arjun could be unapproachable. While she had agreed with him in the morning, it looked like Arjun had mellowed since then. "Mudit mentioned that you have brought your company a long way since you took over."

"Hmm." Arjun pushed his empty plate away before sitting back in his chair. "It was my father who set up the company. I just kept building on it."

It was at least ten times bigger now is what she had heard. "Do you enjoy what you do?"

Arjun gave her a lopsided smile. "Very much."

They chatted for a few minutes before getting up by mutual consent. It was time to get back to work.

A rjun was like a bear with a sore head when he woke up the next morning. It was barely 5.30. He had a quick wash before pulling on a pair of shorts and t-shirt. Wearing socks and track shoes, he stepped out of his flat to run down the stairs all the way from the tenth floor. A jog would definitely help remove the cobwebs from his mind.

He had enjoyed chatting with Kiara during lunch the earlier day. She appeared like a breath of fresh air to his jaded mindset. Unlike the wasted morning, he could get a lot of work done in the afternoon; which was when the thought popped into his mind. *Maybe I should take Kiara out for dinner*. Checking the time to see it was past nine, he got up quickly to walk towards her cabin next door.

"Ms Kiara has left for the day, sir," said Suraj.

Shit! He didn't even have her cell number. "When did she leave?"

"At least an hour back, sir. She left with Mr Mudit."

Arjun's face darkened as he abruptly turned and went back into his cabin, not keen for Suraj at the front office to witness his anger.

Dammit! All women were the same. Two-timing men was a game for them. Arjun had locked his heart against the female sex for ten years. Why the hell had he been tempted to open it once again? Hadn't Jane's betrayal taught him anything at all?

He lifted the ceramic ashtray on his table and threw it at the wall with all his might. Chips of plaster fell off the wall while the ashtray broke into smithereens. Not that Arjun cared. He left his office, planning to take a cab to Lake View Café at the Renaissance Convention Centre Hotel to drown his misery.

After four pegs of Scotch and a *Chicken Baida roll*, Arjun continued to feel melancholic when he caught a cab back home.

Strange dreams dogged him as he spent a restless night and he came wide awake too early.

Jogging around the complex, Arjun was glad there were barely a few stragglers so early in the morning. It was still not light as he pounded his way around, not following any specific route, his mind running over the time he had spent with Kiara.

Were she and Mudit seeing each other? Maybe he should ask his friend upfront. Arjun grimaced as he stopped near a bench, taking deep breaths to calm down his pumping heart as he sat down to take a swig from his water bottle. It was difficult, this strange attraction he felt towards the woman. Why couldn't his heart remain locked up? And safe?

Or maybe it was simple physical chemistry! Could that be what was happening to him? Keeping women at bay had also ensured that Arjun had not had sex in all these years. Maybe his body was clamouring for only sex and his heart wasn't involved in any way.

With a deep sigh, Arjun concluded that he was probably making a mountain out of a molehill.

Unlike Arjun, Kiara woke up late, with a wide smile on her face. The earlier night, she had been out to a film with Mudit and they had stopped at a street food stall and gorged on *cheese pav bhaji* as they chatted about *Tanhaji*, the film they had seen.

"Saif Ali Khan was simply fabulous," declared Kiara, popping a piece of sliced cucumber into her mouth.

"That he was," agreed Mudit. "I only wish there had been more story and less violence."

Kiara nodded, grimacing. "Tell me about it." They had agreed not to talk shop outside of office hours. But she couldn't help asking, "What's Arjun's background?"

Mudit lifted an eyebrow, a teasing expression on his face. "Why do you want to know?"

"*Arre*, I'm interested because I'm working with him." Kiara punched Mudit on his arm. They had chatted for some time during lunch at the canteen. But Arjun hadn't spoken much about himself. And she wanted to know all about him because she found him mind-blowingly hot. Not that she planned to admit all that to Mudit, who was an absolute tease.

Mudit wiggled his eyebrows at her, refusing to say anything as he munched his way through his dinner.

"What? Is he an axe murderer or something?" asked Kiara, tongue-in-cheek.

"Hahaha! I'm not telling."

Kiara pouted at him. "Bastard! I'll find out for myself."

"I'm sure you will, Ms Ethical Hacker."

"But you won't tell me?" She batted her eyelashes, wearing a puppy dog look as she tried to bulldoze him. "Pretty please."

Mudit shook his head as he paid the vendor at the street food stall. "Would you like to drink something? A *gola* maybe?"

"Mudit!" Kiara gave him a reproachful look.

Not waiting for her reply, he ordered two *Kala Khatta* flavoured *golas* before turning to her. "What do you want to know about Arjun?"

"Everything you know."

"Everything? Are you sure?" Mudit gave her a grin.

"Mudit!"

He lifted both his hands in front of him in a gesture of peace. "Okay, okay. Arjun is the only son of Jayant and Anjali Mathur. His father is no more, which you are aware of." He paused when Kiara nodded before continuing, "Jayant Uncle was found murdered in his bed."

"Ouch! When was this?"

Mudit scrunched his eyebrows, thinking. "Almost eleven, maybe twelve years ago. You were probably too young to have read it in the newspapers. Later, his mother got married to Parth Bhardwaj, a famous author who writes under a pseudonym."

"What's the name he uses?" asked Kiara, a curious look on her face.

"Paul Bainsbridge."

"Oh my God! The Paul Bainsbridge! He's Arjun's stepfather?" Kiara's mouth hung open in absolute surprise.

Mudit playfully pressed his forefinger under her chin to close her hanging jaw, laughing at her startled expression. "You have obviously read his books."

"All of them, more than once. Haven't you?"

"But of course. I have got all my copies autographed too."

"You lucky bastard! I'm going to ask Arjun to help me out there."

Mudit sighed.

"What?"

Mudit shook his head at her even as he reached out to take the two glasses of *gola* from the vendor before handing one to Kiara. "Arjun at twenty was a happy young man. It was only later…"

"Was it after his father was murdered?" Kiara's eyes were wide. She was sure it must have affected him badly.

"Surprisingly not. In fact, it was thanks to him that Jayant Uncle's murderer got away with a light sentence."

"What? Are you serious?"

"It's a long story. Maybe for another day. But the cheerful Arjun changed overnight when his girlfriend died."

The colour drained out of Kiara's face. She quickly bent her face down in the pretext of taking out her wallet from her handbag, insisting on paying for the *golas*. If his girlfriend's death had affected Arjun so much, he must have really been in love with her. Was it possible to be jealous of a ghost? Right now, Kiara was.

They got into the cab Mudit flagged down. "How did she die?"

"Jane was in a car accident."

"Hmm." Kiara stopped talking after that, her mind on Arjun.

Mudit didn't mind the silence as he checked his phone for messages. It wasn't long before they reached the lane in Versova where their bungalows were. They got out of the taxi at the corner bungalow where Kiara lived. Once she opened the door with her key, Mudit waved to her before walking back to his house which was two compounds away.

Kiara was thoughtful as she got ready for bed, her mind revolving around Arjun. While he had been aloof in the morning, he had been more friendly during lunch. She wished she knew him well enough to have met him before leaving work. It would have been nice to say 'bye'.

Tomorrow! *Tomorrow*, Kiara promised to herself, *I will get better acquainted with Arjun Mathur.*

Kirit Patel was in a flaming temper as he sat in his sitting room, drinking peg after peg from a bottle of his finest Scotch whiskey. It was almost a week since he had been to work, not from the day he had been thrown out of his post as finance director of Mathur Industries.

If it was in his power, he would have chopped off Arjun Mathur's head and fed it to the dogs. Bastard! If his father Jayant had been a shrewd businessman, the son was in a different league altogether. Jayant had been hands on, keeping an eye on the total running of the company. While Kirit had been working with Mathur Industries for the last fourteen years, it was only after Jayant's death had he been able to make extra money. And that had also been possible only because Arjun had been an absentee boss. It hadn't been difficult to fool old Shiamak Trivedi. Finance was definitely not Shiamak's strength. Kirit had fleeced Mathur Industries to his heart's content, ensuring that the regular thefts could not be traced back to him.

How the hell had Arjun found out that Kirit was siphoning money from the company? Kirit paced the room, round and round, unable to understand. *Where did I go wrong?*

He stopped in his tracks to snap his fingers. Harish! Harish was the man for him. Harish Patel was Kirit's cousin's son, almost as cunning as Kirit himself. The boy's only ambition was to become rich.

Kirit smiled to himself. Harish must have taken after him, even if he was the son of a cousin. He quickly dialled Harish's number and told him to meet him the very next morning.

"But Kirit Uncle, I can't take leave," protested Harish, as if he owed all his loyalty to the furniture company he worked for.

"*Arre*, quit the damn job, my boy. I'll make you a millionaire."

Could he mean it? "Tell me you aren't joking, Uncle." There was a desperate note in Harish's voice.

"If I can't help you earn, I can always make you my *waaris*, can't I?" said Kirit cunningly. He was a rich man with an only daughter who was already married and settled in the USA. His wife Asha was too timid to ask him any questions.

Harish was drooling by now. "Do you want me to come over right now?"

"No, no. Tomorrow should do." Kirit wanted to create a plan before taking his nephew on board.

"I'll see you tomorrow, Kirit Uncle. You are my God!" declared Harish passionately before disconnecting the call.

It had been almost a decade since Harish had broken up with Kiara Bakshi. He had been seeing her for only one reason: that she was the only child of multi-millionaire Chandresh Bakshi.

Well, it hadn't hurt that she was easy on the eye. But one thing about Kiara which Harish couldn't care for at all was that she was too damn innocent. He hadn't even got an opportunity to kiss her.

Idiot!

And another thing he had really hated was the way she admired her father. As if Chandresh Bakshi was God himself! Wasn't it a good thing Harish had chucked her out of his life? No man could compete with a woman's father for attention.

The little fool had been so wrong about her father. Bakshi had been stupid enough to lose all his wealth—a sum close to fifty million rupees—to some online fraud. His bank account had been wiped clean. Only his daughter, Kiara, had got angry with Harish for calling her father a fool. She had actually had the guts to cut his call.

He recalled the scene with clarity even today…

Harish Patel stared at his phone, disbelief on his face when Kiara cut his call. What a little idiot! Older than her by five years, Harish had decided to make her his girlfriend after he met the Bakshi family at a party.

When he noticed the diamonds sparkling on Mrs Bakshi's ears and throat, and the branded suit and 24-carat gold cufflinks which Mr Bakshi sported, Harish made it a point to find out more about them. He wasn't disappointed when he got to know they had a young daughter. He got introduced to Kiara and set about charming her with great enthusiasm though he was smart enough to be subtle about it.

After all, who wouldn't want the beautiful and single child of Chandresh Bakshi as a girlfriend?

He had been surprised at first when he found out that Kiara didn't have a steady boyfriend. Which was before he realised how shy and quiet she was. And there was this obsession she had about her father. Harish admitted to himself that he was jealous of the way Kiara hero-worshipped her parent.

But all that he could tolerate, only because she was born with a golden spoon. Harish knew Chandresh Bakshi was a millionaire many times over, way richer than Harish could probably become in his whole lifetime. And Harish wasn't keen on working hard. There was a rich uncle, his father's cousin Kirit, who had been promising to make Harish his heir. But that might happen sometime in the vague future. Harish had a job in the marketing department of a furniture company and had no ambition other than to get rich quick. What better way than to marry a rich man's only daughter?

He had spent the past eight months wooing Kiara, taking her out every weekend. He was smart enough to encourage her to pay the bills most of the time. And it didn't seem as if she minded. Everything appeared to be going well and Harish was waiting for her to turn eighteen before offering to marry her.

But the news Kiara had shared with him today had shaken him up terribly. If Chandresh Bakshi was stupid enough to lose most of his wealth to an internet hacker, where would that leave Kiara? And Harish for that matter?

Harish decided then and there that he would pursue the second option on his list of rich women. Kiara was of no use to him any longer, not now that she was stripped of all her wealth.

He proceeded to block her on WhatsApp and unfriend her from all his social media profiles. To hell with the had-been heiress. There were more fish in the sea.

But he hadn't found anyone as gullible as Kiara in the whole of a decade. Harish continued to work in the marketing department of the furniture business, not at all keen on the couple of girls his mother had found for him as prospective brides. What was the use of marrying a middle-class woman and leading a middle-class life? He was surely not meant for mediocrity.

At thirty-three, Harish continued to wait for his main chance. Tomorrow, it looked like Kirit Uncle, his father's cousin, was going to give him the chance of a lifetime.

With a wide grin on his face, Harish tossed and turned on his bed throughout the night, too excited to sleep.

Kiara walked into work at ten in the morning. With a plan to get better acquainted with the MD of the company, she walked up to Suraj and asked, "Good morning, Suraj. Is Arjun Mathur in?"

"Yes, Ms Kiara. He's in a meeting though."

"Oh! What about later?"

"Why don't you talk to Chintan Rao? He's Arjun Sir's executive assistant."

"And where will I find this Chintan?"

"The cabin on the other side." Suraj pointed to the one to the left of Arjun's.

Kiara gave a nod, thanked Suraj, and went and knocked on Chintan's door before stepping in. There was a man with salt and pepper hair of indeterminate age, sitting at a desk piled with papers. He lifted calm, grey eyes to hers in query. "Hi, you must be Chintan Rao." When he nodded, she continued, "I'm Kiara Bakshi. I'm a consultant with Mathur Industries."

"I'm aware, Ms Bakshi. Is there anything I can do for you?" He didn't bother to invite her to sit, obviously too busy to spare the time for a chat.

"Yes, please. I would like to meet Arjun Mathur. If you can tell me when that will be possible? I hear he's in a meeting now."

Chintan quickly looked at his phone to check his boss's appointments. "You can see the MD after eight when his last meeting would be done."

"What?" Kiara's eyes went wide in surprise. The earlier day, Arjun had seemed quite free. She had assumed he had enough people working for him, running the business on oiled wheels rather than toil hard himself. But today seemed to be a different day altogether. She also admitted to a feeling of acute disappointment. "There's no small window between two meetings? I just need a couple of minutes."

"I can check, Ms Bakshi. But I can't promise." Chintan tilted his head. "I'll call you on your extension if such a window appears, I promise."

"Great. Thanks, Chintan. I'll wait for your call." Not having a choice, she left his cabin to cross Arjun's door on the way to her office, not missing the murmur of voices from within, even if she couldn't hear anything intelligible.

She walked into her cabin and began to work, soon too engrossed to be bothered about anything else. It was past 2.30 pm when Mudit invited her to the canteen for lunch. There had been no call from Chintan and it was obvious that Arjun was in yet another meeting when Kiara left her office to go down to the twelfth floor where the canteen was. She returned after a quick lunch, too keen to catch the discrepancies in the accounting.

It was past eight when she shut her laptop, lifting her arms above her head to stretch luxuriously. Should she simply barge into Arjun's office? Following action to thought, Kiara immediately stepped out of her cabin to walk over to Arjun's.

"Arjun sir has left for the day, Ms Kiara." Suraj called out to her from where he was locking his desk. "Will you be staying long?"

"Huh?!" Kiara shook her head as if to clear it, not sure if she had heard him right. Chintan had promised to call her when Arjun was free. But she had received no such call. How could Arjun simply leave before she could speak to him? "Tch!" She suddenly looked up at Suraj who was waiting for her reply. "No, Suraj. I'll leave in five minutes."

Sura gave her a nod before continuing with what he had been doing.

"Has Chintan left?" she turned around to ask Suraj.

"Not yet, ma'am."

Kiara turned right back and walked over to Chintan's cabin, knocking on the door before entering. "Hello again, Chintan."

"Hello Ms Bakshi. I'm sorry but the MD left immediately after his last meeting got over."

"I thought as much. How busy is he tomorrow?" Maybe she should take an appointment as well.

"He's not in office the whole of tomorrow morning. You can meet him at, say, 4 pm. Works for you?" Chintan looked up from the appointment calendar to ask her.

"It will have to work," she said, giving the executive assistant a charming smile. "Thanks, Chintan. I'll see you tomorrow."

Chintan gave a nod, saying, "Good night, Ms Bakshi."

"You must call me Kiara." She turned from the door to tell him before leaving the cabin. Talk about being elusive. Arjun Mathur definitely was. Which only made Kiara all the more determined to see him the next day.

That day at work, Arjun had back-to-back meetings and had no time to even think of Kiara. In fact, he was so tied up that he managed to grab a bite of sandwich and a cup of tea for lunch which his executive assistant, Chintan Rao, provided him with, in between meetings.

It was almost seven when Arjun opened his cell phone to check for messages. Ignoring the WhatsApp messages from twenty-odd people, he zeroed in on the one from a friend.

Hey Arjun. Want to go for a swim?

The message was from Krish Sanyal, a close friend from his university days at Kingston. Over the years, they had kept in touch, meeting on and off whenever they were in the same city. Krish was a travel photographer and roamed the world. He also touched base in Mumbai on and off.

Sure, why not? You wanna pop over to my building society? Arjun quickly typed with both his thumbs as he leaned back in his chair, exhausted.

I'm staying at The Fern in Acres Club. Why don't you come over as my guest? was Krish's reply.

Will see you in an hour. Arjun signed off, looking forward to spending the evening with Krish. Acres Club was in Chembur and it would take him some time to get there. He immediately left the office to drive home, forgetting all about Kiara and Mudit.

He booked a cab after taking a shower as they would probably end up drinking more than a peg or two.

"What's up, *mere yaar*?" asked Krish, grinning widely at Arjun, his light brown eyes twinkling with mirth. He was extremely cheerful by nature and enjoyed his bohemian lifestyle. No one looking at Krish would believe that he worked extremely hard and was super rich.

"All going good," said Arjun, sipping from his drink—whiskey and soda—which was set on a tray next to the pool. It was beautifully quiet as there wasn't much of a crowd on a Tuesday night and they had just completed twenty rigorous laps of the long pool. It had been thoroughly invigorating. "How's Dip?" Dipika was Krish's younger sister who ran a modelling agency. Krish helped with the photography whenever he was in town.

"She's good, happy. How's Anjali Aunty? And Parth?"

Arjun smiled. "Both are awesome, writing up a storm. Can you believe my Mom has sold more than a million copies of her books?" Arjun couldn't help the note of pride which slipped into his voice.

"Whoa! That's simply amazing, Arjun. You must be so proud of her."

Arjun nodded. "You bet! So, which part of the world are you coming from?"

"Australia. I did a series on the aborigines and travelled all around. It makes such a fascinating study. The way they connect to the earth and the animals is so amazing." Krish spoke for a long while about the video series he was shooting for the National Geographic Channel.

Arjun listened, totally rivetted. It was late when they had dinner.

"Why don't you bunk along with me instead of going all the way home?" Krish lifted an enquiring brow at Arjun.

Arjun shook his head, grimacing. "It'd be easier to get home at this hour rather than in the morning. And tomorrow is another long day at work." He got up, giving his friend a hug before stepping towards the gate where a cab was waiting for him. "Are you in Mumbai for long? We could meet again."

"Not sure. Will ping you."

Lifting his hand in a wave, Arjun got into the cab, feeling more cheerful than he had been in the morning. With a long-drawn sigh, he decided it would be for the best if he stayed away from Kiara. She was cute and chirpy. But that didn't mean she was any better than other women.

Arjun was better off in his single status!

Kiara was wrapped in a bath towel as she checked herself out in the mirror the next morning. She wiggled her eyebrows at herself, pouting her lips. Not bad! Her face was a perfect oval, her eyes big and black with thick and curling lashes being her best feature. Okay, there were times when she wished her eyelashes were longer, but they would do, she thought, fluttering them rapidly. Her cheeks were smooth while her pert nose was tilted at the tip. Her lips! Well, they could have been a little less wide, but so what? Kiara shrugged her slender shoulders. She liked her face. With a touch of foundation, eyeliner, and lipstick, it looked almost beautiful.

What Kiara didn't realise was that her face was too damn cute. That was probably because she saw it every day and took it for granted. And she also wasn't the kind of person who was all that bothered about her appearance. She was too involved with her career and all her time and energy went into focussing on it.

Today, she decided not to wear her regular work uniform of jeans, shirt, and cotton jacket. If she wanted to grab Arjun's attention, she needed to wear something different, something eye catching. It wasn't as if she didn't have the latest clothes in her wardrobe. But then, it had to be something which would fit in with the office atmosphere.

Running through the colourful dresses, skirts, pants, and tops in her wardrobe, she quickly pulled out a pastel yellow, hip length tunic top which was embroidered at the neck, hem and sleeve in a deep shade of green and red. She wore a pair of form fitting rich cream linen, form fitting, full pants with it, cinching the pants at the waist with a wide cloth belt of the same shade of cream. She turned this way and that to check herself in the floor-length mirror.

Yes! Kiara pumped a fist in the air before quickly walking out of her bedroom and running down the stairs to the dining room.

"Good morning, Papa, Mama," she called out cheerfully, giving her mother a hug before turning around to kiss her father's cheek.

"Good morning, *Beta*. Are you going to work today or are you on holiday?" asked Chandresh, eyeing his daughter's attire with a smile on his face.

"Good morning, Kiara. I was going to ask the same thing," said Kalpana, grinning as she sat next to her husband at the dining table.

"Is it too loud?" asked Kiara, tucking into the *chole bhature* the cook had made for breakfast.

"Not loud exactly. But it isn't what you usually wear," said her mother, sipping from a tall glass of *sweet lassi*.

"That it isn't." Kiara agreed with Kalpana.

"So, who's your target?" asked her father.

"Huh?!" Kiara gave Chandresh a startled glance. Was it so obvious she was targeting a man, trying to get his attention? Following the thought, she immediately realised her father was just asking a simple question, without any ulterior motive.

"I mean who do you plan to target with your power dressing?" Chandresh sat back to drink his *lassi* as well.

Kiara liked to eat slowly, taking half an hour to finish her breakfast. This way, she felt her digestive system worked way better and her energy levels always remained high. "Hahaha! Nothing like that. I was feeling bored with jeans and shirts. Felt like some colour. You sure it's not gaudy, no? Mama?"

Kalpana shook her head, laughing. "For a young woman, I don't think you have anything gaudy in your wardrobe, especially considering we are Punjabis." She felt that her daughter should wear more colourful clothes.

"That's fine then. Anyone for *chai*?" Kiara preferred hot tea to the cold *lassi* which she felt made her lethargic.

Both her parents shook their heads even as Dara Singh, the cook, brought a pot of tea and placed it in front of Kiara.

"Thank you so much, Dara Uncle," said Kiara, giving him a wide smile.

"You are welcome, baby," said the cook who had been working with the Bakshi family from the time even before Kiara was born.

Kiara had two cups of *masala chai*, relishing it thoroughly. "I'll be off then. Need to leave in ten minutes."

"Will you be going with Mudit?" asked Kalpana. She secretly hoped Kiara and Mudit would get together. Her daughter was twenty-seven and showed no signs of interest in any young man. Kiara had made it clear she wouldn't have an arranged marriage. What irked Kalpana was the way Chandresh supported his daughter in anything and everything. All the relatives seemed to nag only Kalpana, pointing out that she had failed as a mother to get her daughter married at the right time.

"No, Mama. Mudit goes too early." Kiara shuddered. "I prefer to leave *aaram se*."

A proud smile lit up Chandresh's face as he watched his daughter racing up the stairs. Kiara was the best. She had not only mastered hacking techniques, but also got all his stolen money back. And now, she single-handedly ran a flourishing business catching crooks and making pots of money in the bargain. He wanted only the best for his Kiara. If she wanted to get married a few years later, so be it. Or if she wanted to spend all her life with her parents, he wouldn't mind that either. All he wanted was for Kiara to be happy.

On the other hand, Kalpana looked at her daughter's retreating figure with a small frown puckering her neatly plucked eyebrows. Of course, she appreciated that Kiara had a wonderful career which she was passionate about. She even admired the hard work she put in. But how could only a career be enough for a girl? Didn't she need a husband? And children? At least one? As for Kalpana and Chandresh, they would have had more kids, only the doctor had warned them that Kalpana's uterus wasn't strong enough to bear another child. She sighed now.

"What's wrong, Kalpana?" Chandresh asked his wife when he heard her sigh.

"When will our daughter get married?" Kalpana almost wailed.

"When she meets the right man." Chandresh pacified his wife, a hand on her shoulder.

Kalpana rolled her eyes. "And how is she going to meet the right man? What do you think of Mudit? Won't he make Kiara a good husband?"

"You want our daughter to marry a Gujarati boy?" Chandresh asked his wife teasingly. Personally, he wouldn't give a damn what religion his son-in-law belonged to.

"As long as she gets married to a suitable young man, does it matter what religion he is from?" Kalpana gave her husband a desperate look. "It's all because of you, Chandresh. You spoil her too much, letting her run scot free. Kiara is twenty-seven. At her age, I was mother to a seven-year-old." She sniffed, all set to cry.

Chandresh got up from his chair. "Listen, Kalpana. Those times were different. Your parents prepared you to become a housewife. But we haven't brought up Kiara that way. Let her enjoy her freedom, *na*? What's the hurry?"

"All our relatives are laughing behind our backs," she grumbled, piling the empty plates one on top of the other.

"Are they? Ask them if they have the guts to laugh in front of our faces."

"Everything is a joke for you."

"Hahaha! You take life too seriously, Kalpana. Want to go to a movie?"

Kalpana stared at her husband, her mouth wide open. "Don't you need to go to work?"

"I feel like taking the day off." At fifty-nine, Chandresh led a relaxed life. When all his money got stolen from his account, he had had a lot of time to think and reconsider his priorities. He had made a conscious decision not to take things too seriously. Life needed to be savoured, enjoyed. It was not all about existing, but living every moment to the full.

When Kiara rushed down the stairs, with her make up on, Kalpana gave her a wide smile. Maybe, her daughter would meet someone interesting today.

"Your mother and I are off to watch a film."

"Wow! That's awesome, Papa. Which one?"

"*Tanhaji*."

Kiara grimaced. "It's too violent, Papa. I don't think Mama will like it."

"You think I enjoy violence?" asked Chandresh, tongue-in-cheek.

Kiara laughed. "You're right. You wouldn't either. Hmm… there's *Panga*, a sports drama."

"What do reviews say?" asked Chandresh, picking up his phone to check.

"All good only. Have fun, both of you. I'll see you guys later."

"Bye *Beta*." Chandresh called out to his daughter as she rushed out of the front door.

"Be careful, Kiara," said her mother, her lips turned down at the corners.

"Okay, let's give Kiara six months. If she doesn't find herself a husband, we'll look for one." Chandresh aim was to only pacify his wife.

"Promise?" Kalpana's face lit up with a bright smile.

"Promise," said her husband, kissing her on her forehead.

It was 3.45 and Kiara was thoroughly impatient. She had already been to check if Arjun was back from wherever the hell he had been to. She had even refused to go down for lunch and had ordered something in her office.

The job which had excited her all these years, seemed so flat today. Where was the MD of Mathur Industries? She stepped out of her office for the fifth time when she saw him walk out of the elevator.

"Hello Mr Mathur," she called out.

Arjun turned around with a dark frown to see who it was who had stopped him in his tracks. No one had dared, not in the past decade or longer. The frown didn't leave his face when he eyed Kiara. The jeans and jacket were gone and in their place were some sort of… well, he couldn't really complain as her clothes were suitable office attire. But why the hell did she have to appear so sexy? "Yes, Ms Bakshi. Did you want something?"

Bear! That was what he was, *a bear with a sore head.* The time they had spent at the office canteen, chatting away while he had lunch, seemed to have been forgotten. With an effort, Kiara stopped herself from giving a loud snort. Taking a deep breath, she said, "I need a few minutes of your time."

"Alright. Come over," he said, walking into his office.

She made a face before following him right inside, not bothering to wait for his invitation before sitting down in one of the chairs in front of his desk.

Arjun removed his suit jacket and draped it over the back of his chair before loosening his tie, totally unaware of the effect he was having on the woman in front of him. As for his concentration on removing his cufflinks, he was taking a lot of time over it as he was working hard at trying to get back his lost breath. The ethical hacker Mudit had introduced him to was not only beautiful, but too damn sexy. Arjun took his own sweet time before settling down in his chair, striking a relaxed pose as he lifted an eyebrow at her. "Tell me."

Kiara pressed her lips together, scared of what might come out of her mouth. He was dishy, to put it in one word, what with the five o'clock shadow darkening his lean cheeks and his oh-so-kissable mouth. He had opened the top two buttons of his shirt and she could see the strong pulse beating steadily at his throat; and the upper portion of his broad chest which had a smattering of dark hair. His forearms were exposed as he had pushed his shirt sleeves back, only a silver watch adorning his left wrist, his large hands placed on the arms of his swivel chair, the fingers long with neatly trimmed nails. That sure was a turn-on for her; long fingers, and well-trimmed nails.

Uff!

Kiara felt a sudden urge to fan herself as the heat quotient had suddenly upped in the room despite the coolness of the air-conditioning.

According to his executive assistant, Arjun had been out at meetings all morning but there was no trace of tiredness on his handsome face. She realised she could watch him all day without feeling bored, not one little bit.

"Ms Bakshi?" He wanted to glare at the silent woman in front of him, only his face refused to cooperate. She was such a lovely sight to behold, so much so that he wanted to smile at her. But Arjun being Arjun, clamped his lips together and refused to allow them to stretch into a smile.

"Kiara. The name is Kiara," she said, her voice a hoarse whisper as she saw him struggling not to smile. Then suddenly, she grinned at him, her whole face lighting up. "I'm going to call you Arjun."

That was it! No by-your-leave. She had simply declared that she was going to call him by his first name. And why the hell did his stomach have to take a leap in reaction? He gave a nod, without saying a word as he wasn't sure if his vocal cords would cooperate with him, not with his heart taking residence in his throat, closing it off completely.

Just then, Chintan entered with a tray which contained a plate with a sandwich and two cups of coffee. "I thought Kiara might like some coffee too," said Chintan, placing the tray on the table.

"Thanks, Chintan, that's so sweet of you." Kiara gave the executive assistant a broad smile.

But what surprised Arjun was the answering smile on the dour Chintan's face as he gave her a nod, saying, "You are welcome, Kiara. Do you need anything else, Arjun?" Chintan asked his boss as an afterthought.

"No, I'm good. Thanks, Chintan. And you may leave for the day if you want to. You've been working too many long hours lately." The truth was that Arjun wanted his executive assistant as far away from Kiara as was possible. Chintan may be on the wrong side of thirty and not all that good-looking, but Arjun didn't miss the warmth the man shared with Kiara. How the hell had it happened? Chintan didn't like people, period. Or was that a façade?

"That would be great. In that case, I'd like to leave in half an hour."

"Sure. I'll see you tomorrow then." Once Chintan left, Arjun turned to look at Kiara once again. "Would you like a bite of sandwich?" he asked, handing her a steaming coffee mug.

"Not for me. I had my lunch barely a couple of hours back."

Nodding, he took a bite of the sandwich, his eyes roaming over her face. It was as if he had suddenly lost control of all his senses. "Go on. What did you want to talk to me about?"

"Just that I should be done with my investigations in another three days. I have collected most of the evidence, the money trail and all."

Arjun's hand stopped on its way to his mouth, the sandwich quarter held in his fingers, completely forgotten. "Are you saying you will be done in barely a week since you began?" He was not just astounded, but absolutely impressed.

Light colour ran up Kiara's face when she heard his words. She shrugged, trying to make light of the situation. "Well, to be truthful, the thieves haven't really been all that smart."

"Are you saying there is more than one thief?" Arjun somehow managed to focus on eating his food as he asked the question.

"Of course. There rarely is one person involved in such an elaborate operation. Help is required to make sure the transactions can't be traced back to one person. It's usually a syndicate. In this case, it's three people. At least, I have traced three people so far. There might be more by the end of it."

Arjun grimaced. "Do all of them work for me?"

"No, Arjun. Only one of them does. The others are all outsiders."

"Phew! At least that's a relief." He lifted the coffee mug to sip from it. "So, what happens now?"

"I need access to some more files. Mudit says only you can grant me the permission. And there's also the need to bring the cyber cell on board soon."

"Hmm. Will you send me an email, copy to Mudit, regarding what all you need access to?"

"Sure. I'll send you the mail right away." She gave him another dazzling smile, making his heart flip over.

Arjun gritted his teeth, irritated with himself. But before he could get a control over himself, he asked, "Will you have dinner with me?" While he regretted the words the moment they left his lips, he wasn't at all keen to withdraw them.

"I'd love to," she said, grinning by now. It looked like the change of clothes had worked wonders.

"Right then. Let's leave at seven. Will you be done by then?"

"Even if I'm not, I'll shut my laptop. I'm not going to miss the chance to have dinner with you." Kiara laughed as she got up from her chair. "I'll see you soon." With a wave, she left Arjun's cabin, leaving him dazed.

Had he heard right? Or were his ears playing tricks on him? Kiara was keen to have dinner with him. Had he made a mistake inviting her out? Would she read something more than what was on offer?

And what exactly was on offer? Arjun had no plans of opening his heart to her. No way. All he was ready to do was spend a couple of hours with her, having dinner and talking, maybe what he would do with Mudit or Krish.

And who was he fooling?

Kiara was an attractive woman who made his nerves jump every time she came within a few feet of him. What she did to his heart, he wasn't even going to acknowledge. He was just going to spend some time with her.

That was it!

With that thought firmly entrenched in his mind, Arjun got up to leave. He needed a shower. No way was he going to take a lady out for dinner, not after a sweaty visit to his factory.

Kiara had a difficult time not letting her mouth fall open when she saw Arjun later in the evening. He had obviously had a shower and change of clothes, looking natty in a pair of dark blue jeans, a pristine white shirt, and a powder blue linen jacket. His longish hair had been combed back, the ends touching the back of his neck. While he looked even handsomer than before, Kiara missed the fuzz on his cheeks which he had sported earlier. Now, his face was clean shaven.

"Are you ready to leave?" Arjun stood at the entrance to her cabin, leaning casually against the doorway, his arms folded against his wide and muscular chest. It was difficult to hold himself back as all he wanted to do was to pull her out of her chair and into his arms. Would his self-control last till the end of the day? Somehow, Arjun wasn't too confident. As his eyes roved over her lovely features, he didn't miss the fact that her face was neatly made up, her lips glowing a soft peach colour. She was also wearing some kind of dangling earrings which hadn't been there when she had gone to his cabin a while back.

"In a minute. I'm just locking up." She got up from her chair, sliding her feet into a pair of open-toed-wedges the exact shade of cream as her pants.

"You can leave your laptop here if you want to."

Kiara was shaking her head even before he finished speaking. "I work at all kind of hours. I'd rather it went with me," she said, walking towards him, her handbag on her right shoulder and her laptop case in her left hand. "You look so smart! You make me wonder if I should have…"

Arjun laughed, unable to stop himself as he reached out to take her laptop case. Running his eyes from the top of her head to the tips of her toes peeping through the wedges, he said, "It was because of how lovely you look that I rushed home to have a shower and change. I didn't want to appear shabby beside you, not for our dinner date." His voice was rough as his heart beat an unsteady but rapid tattoo, his hands itching to run through the corkscrew curls which fell in a cute disarray all over her shoulders.

"Huh?!" Kiara gave him a wide-eyed look, searching his face to see if he was teasing her. "Come on, Arjun. You don't have to flatter me. I'm not "lovely"; not by any stretch of the imagination." She shook her head at him, her curls tumbling all the more as she drew quotation marks in the air.

Was she fishing for more compliments? Arjun wasn't sure. He realised he had really no idea how to deal with a young woman, not having spent any time with one, not in the past decade. Only, Kiara didn't seem the type, not with the kind of confidence she projected.

But she must definitely be expecting some kind of a response from him. He waited for her to get into the elevator before stepping inside. "I don't know what kind of men you have been seeing. Half blind ones maybe?" He lifted an eyebrow at her.

Kiara shook her head at him, soft colour glowing on her cheeks even as a smile curved her lips.

"Unless they are all fully blind."

She burst out laughing. More than finding his words funny, she was simply thrilled she was going out with the smartest and most attractive man she had ever met. Yes, in that order! It was his intelligence which made him so appealing.

Bracing himself for the impact, Arjun took her elbow in his hand when the lift doors slid open. But nothing had prepared him for the shock waves which hit his nerves from his palm and fingers, all the way up his arm and shoulder. What was with this woman? Even when he was living with Jane, he didn't remember ever feeling such a powerful sensation, not once. Was it because of the years of abstinence? He hadn't touched a woman, not since Jane, not with the tip of his finger; which was probably the reason.

He couldn't deny that Kiara was growing on him, most definitely. Was he in for one more horrible experience, a heart break maybe? How could he save himself from getting hurt? Could he keep his heart and emotions out of the equation and simply have some fun?

Taking a deep breath, Arjun clenched his jaw, determined to give it a try.

Kiara felt his hand at her elbow and didn't miss the heat of his touch right through the silky material of her tunic. It was with an effort she stopped herself from leaning her head on his shoulder as she walked along with him to the glass doors at the front of the office building. A valet had brought his car around, a shiny black BMW Benz. It reminded her of a sleek panther, not all that different from its owner.

"Ooh! This is lovely," she exclaimed, running a hand over its smooth exterior.

Arjun gulped when he felt a kick to his solar plexus as he studied her slender hand tracing the side of his car. He waved away the valet who rushed forward to open the door and did the honours himself, handing her into the passenger seat before walking around the bonnet. He slipped into the driver's seat and pulled the safety belt across to lock it in place. "Are you comfortable? Or would you like me to adjust your seat?"

I would like you to do a number of things for me! Kiara bit back her tongue to stop the words from spilling out. Instead, "It's perfect," she said, lowering her gaze which glowed with excitement as she studied the leather upholstery in a soft shade of beige. "Is it new?"

He turned to her, not having heard her words as he concentrated on sliding the car smoothly away from the entrance to ride it towards the main gate. "I'm sorry. What did you ask?"

"Is it new? Your car?"

He shrugged, turning left outside the gate. "It's almost three years old."

"Oh!" It looked as good as new. He must be maintaining it really well.

"Where would you like to go? Any specific cuisine you like?"

"Chinese," she declared immediately before lowering her voice to a near whisper, "but the Indian kind, if you know what I mean. I don't much care for the original bland variety."

"Hahaha! I know exactly what you mean and completely agree with you. So, let me see. Would you like to go to 5 Spice?"

Kiara's stomach rumbled loudly in response, cracking her up. She laughed and laughed before saying breathlessly, "I don't know about me but my tummy agrees with you."

Arjun couldn't help the smile which stretched across his face. Her laughter was too damn infectious.

"Do you want me to book a table?" she offered, having finally recovered her breath.

"Could you do that?"

She quickly checked for the number on the internet and dialled the Vile Parle outlet to find out that the waiting was for an hour and a half. The Bandra outlet informed her that she could get a table for two in about an hour. She promised to call them back before hanging up on each of them. Quickly explaining the waiting time to him, she asked, "What do you think?"

"Go ahead and book a table at the Vile Parle outlet. We'll go somewhere for a drink and later to the restaurant. Works for you?"

"Sure," she said, quickly dialling the Vile Parle 5 Spice and booking a table for two for nine o'clock.

Arjun quickly drove to The Lalit, all the traffic in the opposite direction. Handing the car keys to a valet, he escorted her to Beluga, the hotel's bar which was at the lobby level.

They sat across each other on the sofas close to the long windows facing the fountain. Kiara didn't like the distance between them. There was a long table between the sofas. Agreed it was low and she could still see him, but he was so far away. Gritting her teeth, she decided to grin and bear it.

As for Arjun, he was glad of the space. He wasn't sure what he would have done if he was sitting next to her. His libido seemed to have woken up with a vengeance.

A waiter brought a couple of menus and handed them over. Arjun waved him away before asking her, "Are you a wine kind of person or do you prefer hard liquor?"

"I'm so glad you asked. I simply hate wine." She wrinkled her nose, making her appear all the cuter to the man sitting opposite her. She quickly ran her finger down the list and asked, "Are you fond of beer?"

"You are?" he asked.

"I love it," she said, smacking her lips, inadvertently driving him crazy with the action.

"I'll ask for a pitcher. What say?"

She nodded vigorously, her curls dancing about her face.

Arjun placed the order for a draught pitcher of beer. "I'm sure we could have some starters. You are hungry."

"That I am," she said, grinning as she ran through the food menu. "Do you recommend something?"

"Something spicy and non-veg?" He tried to guess her taste.

"Perfect. Just what I need right now."

Arjun turned to the waiter and said, "Bring us a portion of Chilli Garlic Prawns."

"Sure, sir," said the waiter, leaving to place their orders with the bar and the kitchen.

Soon, Arjun found himself in the strangest of circumstances, swigging beer with a woman who actually looked like a college student, her laughter ringing out every other minute. He felt his heart swell with joy, even as worry niggled him at the very back of his mind.

What if?!

Unaware of the undercurrents bothering Arjun, Kiara had the time of her life as they chatted about this and that, the conversation flowing comfortably. What if she spoke a hundred words to his dozen? She really didn't care as long as she got to spend time with him.

In the end, they cancelled their table at the 5 Spice Restaurant as they had had three more starters and one more pitcher of beer.

"I'm simply too full," said Kiara, pushing away her empty plate.

"So am I."

When it was time to go, Arjun called a car driver service and hired a man to drive them home.

They settled in the back before the car took off. Kiara turned to look at the man she was deeply attracted to. He was seated too far away from her and too close to the window on his side as if he was avoiding her proximity. *Was he?*

Arjun fisted his hands, praying for control. All he wanted was to pull her into his arms and make wild love to her. But where would they go from there? Would she be interested in a casual affair, with no strings attached? For that matter, will he be able to get out of the affair, his heart whole? The anatomy in question beat hard, even trying to jump into his throat, on the verge of choking him when he felt Kiara's hand on his.

She took his left hand in hers, studying the contrast. His hand was almost double the size of hers and way more bronzed while her skin was pale. When he didn't pull away, she flipped over his hand and stared at the strong lines which crisscrossed over his palm. Oh, the long fingers! How she would love to have them run all over her body! Kiara shut her eyes before taking deep breaths to calm down, curbing the temptation to press a kiss into his palm. It was simply too soon.

Unable to stop himself, Arjun wrapped her slender hand in his, pressing his palm to hers, his blood sizzling at the contact. He turned towards her, their eyes clinging to each other, unable to pull away.

The driver honked suddenly and the moment was lost. Arjun pulled his hand away, already regretting his behaviour. *What's come over me?*

Kiara glared at the back of the driver's head. What terrible timing! Before she could say something, they arrived at her bungalow. She wanted to kick at something as she quickly opened the door to get out of the car. With a mammoth effort, she shut the door quietly instead of slamming it as her instinct screamed. She quickly walked around the boot to reach the gate only to find Arjun holding it open for her, her forgotten laptop bag in his hand.

She stepped into the compound, refusing to look at him. She wasn't sure if she wouldn't throw herself into his arms if she looked into his honey brown gaze just now. Stopping at her door, she took the key from her handbag and opened it only to find his hand on her arm.

"Kiara..."

"Hmm..." She turned towards him, even now refusing to look up at his face.

"Thanks for the lovely evening. I don't know about you, but I had a great time." His voice was a soft whisper close to her ear, his breath brushing the tendrils of hair lying against her cheek, bringing her out in goose bumps.

Her handbag slid down to the floor as Kiara reached out to cup his face in both her hands before pressing her lips to the right corner of his mouth. She drew in a deep breath, savouring the unique smell of Arjun—something all male and woodsy—which went to her head like potent whiskey. It was a wonder that she didn't simply melt and slide down to the floor.

Arjun didn't know what hit him when he felt the warmth of her hands holding his face. And then to top that sensation, the kiss at the corner of his lips… it was mind blowing. But before he could react, she let go of him, walked into her home, and shut the door firmly behind her. He stood there for a few moments, totally dazed. The high he had been on, with all the beer he had consumed, was gone for a toss. His body was taut now, like a tightly coiled spring. He did an about turn and walked to the waiting car. Time for a cold shower and it didn't really matter it was almost two in the morning. Not if he wanted to get at least a few hours of sleep.

Kiara leaned against the shut door; her ears tuned in to Arjun's movements outside. She waited to hear him walk away, her heart thudding and wasn't really surprised when there was no noise from outside. It was a while before she heard his footsteps receding away from her door. She stepped out of her shoes before taking a deep breath and tiptoeing her way up the staircase.

She didn't know nor did she care what he thought of her behaviour. But she wouldn't do it differently if she was given another chance. Her mouth still tingled as she recalled the moment when she had pressed it to his face. She only wished she had been bolder and kissed him properly, on his lips.

With a mischievous grin, Kiara removed her clothes and walked into the bathroom for a shower.

Next time, she promised herself.

Sleep refused to come as Kiara tossed and turned on her bed, a smile on her lips as she ruminated over the time she had spent with Arjun. It had been such a wonderful evening.

She couldn't help recalling the time when she had dated Harish, her first boyfriend. He had been good looking and knew exactly the right things to tell the seventeen-year-old innocent who had been floored by his flattering words.

But when she had been in trouble, he had simply disappeared from her life. Wasn't it a good thing she had been more irritated than hurt?

She remembered her feelings when Harish had insulted her father over the phone. He had called her father a fool for having lost all the money in his bank account. Too angry for words, she had simply disconnected his call which had led to both of them cutting each other out of their lives. She hadn't needed to do much as Harish had blocked her everywhere on social media and even his WhatsApp.

Good riddance to bad rubbish!

She remembered that night like now, the night when her whole life had been transformed…

After cutting the call, Kiara stared at her phone in anger. Harish had seemed so nice. Too young to feel tied down by a boyfriend, she had enjoyed being the centre of his attention and even the times they went out. And she really hadn't minded footing the bills every time as it was obvious she had a lot of money while Harish had to slog for the mediocre salary he earned.

Harish was good-looking, smart, and seemed nice. More than all that, he had pursued Kiara relentlessly and the young lady had been totally flattered by the attention of a guy who was five years older than her. To a seventeen-year-old young woman, the attention of a twenty-two-year-old man was simply too tempting to resist.

Just now she wondered what she had ever seen in him. To begin with, he was a miser. So, what if he was good-looking? How dare Harish call her father a fool? Her father who was such an intelligent businessman? Her father who loved both his wife and daughter with all his heart?

As for Harish, he had broken off relations with his parents and two siblings. Or that was what he had told her. He obviously had no sense of family value.

Kiara shrugged. It had been fun hanging out with him all this long. It was time to move on. Maybe, she might even enjoy her single status.

With that thought in mind, she went to sleep with a smile on her face. As for the financial crisis which had shaken the family so horribly, Kiara wasn't too worried. She was going to help her father in his business from now on. And she was also going to find a way to recover the lost money.

The next morning, Kiara woke up at seven to boot her laptop immediately. After a wash and a cup of coffee she took from the kitchen where the cook was already preparing breakfast, she did a lot of reading on the internet and found all she could about ethical hacking—the black hats, the white hats and the grey hats as well.

She was going to find the thief and make him pay, by hook or by crook. Kiara decided then and there that she was going to become a hacking specialist and even signed up for an online course on the same.

The three of them—Kiara and her parents—sat down to breakfast as usual. Noticing her father's haggard face, Kiara placed a hand on his arm, saying, "I'm going to find the thief, Papa. You should stop worrying right now."

Chandresh placed his hand over her small one, giving her a sad smile. "No *Beta*. You stay away from these shady characters. I don't want you to land in any kind of trouble. Let the police and the cyber cell handle the matter. I've been thinking… if they don't come up with a lead in a week or so, I'm planning to hire a private detective to find out more."

With a determined thrust to her chin, Kiara declared, "I have signed up for a basic course in ethical hacking, Papa. If I am able to grasp things, I plan to do an advance course as well." What she didn't say was how determined she was to excel in both the basic and advance levels.

Chandresh sipped on his coffee, eyeing his daughter lovingly. "Are you sure, Kiara? Do you want to wait until I find out more about this ethical hacking you are talking about?"

"I'll be eighteen in three months, Papa. I'm not a child anymore. And I know what I'm talking about." With the exuberance of youth, Kiara polished off the two *paneer gobi parathas* on her plate, sipping from a second cup of tea.

Chandresh gave his nod with a smile on his face.

And that was how she had got out of the situation, heart whole and triumphant as she successfully mastered the basics of ethical hacking and went to do an advance course too.

Two temporary and not so appealing boyfriends later, here she was, on the brink of falling headlong in love.

Her eyes firmly shut while her lips stretched in a wide smile, Kiara turned on her bed yet again, hugging a pillow close to her body. Arjun hadn't objected when she took his hand in his. In fact, he had returned the gesture by holding her palm against his own. And as for Kiara kissing him, he hadn't pulled away.

It was obvious something was bothering the MD of Mathur Industries. And Mudit probably knew all about it. She will have to pump her childhood friend for more information. Kiara plumped her pillows and buried her face in them, willing sleep to claim her.

As for Arjun, the cold shower hadn't helped at all. Every time he thought of the woman who seemed to have a strange grip on his heart, he broke out in goose bumps. He recalled every single word she had uttered, every expression on her vivacious face as she chattered her way through the evening until late night. Her laughter had rung out so often, making him smile. He couldn't remember smiling as much as last night, not ever in his life.

She was wonderful company. And he couldn't wait to see her again. Picking the phone from the table next to his bed, he sent her a message.

Can we meet for breakfast tomorrow? Today actually. He added a smiley face for good measure.

Her reply came almost immediately.

Yes, would love to. But hope not too early; which was followed by a wink smiley.

Let's do brunch then, around 11-12. What say?

I say YES. U unable to sleep?

Hmm

His phone rang and he couldn't stop the feeling of excitement which made his heart hammer in his chest when he saw her face on the screen. Picking the call immediately he said, "Hi, you unable to sleep either?"

"Yep."

"We probably overdid the beer," he declared.

"You wanna hear the truth?" She waited a few moments, and continued when there was no sound from his end, "I'm suffering from unrequited attraction. I…"

"What?" *Did I hear that right?* Arjun took the phone off his ear and stared at it in confusion bordering on astonishment, before asking, "What did you say?"

"You heard me. In case I haven't made myself clear, I am attracted to you and it's unrequited. So… you know what I mean."

His whole body responded to her voice, her words, with alacrity, laying waste to the damned cold shower he had taken in the middle of the chilly January night. "Are you sure it's unrequited?" he asked in a hoarse whisper.

"You tell me." Kiara pressed a hand over her skipping heart, breathlessly waiting for his response.

Arjun cleared his throat. There was only one way to go—forward. "I'm deeply attracted to you too, Kiara. The truth is I had a difficult time keeping my hands off you…"

"Yes!" Kiara jumped out of her bed to pump her fist in the air, grinning from ear to ear. "I knew it!"

"You did?" Arjun lay back in his bed, enjoying his middle-of-the-night phone call.

"Yep! What do we do about it?" she asked, walking to her balcony, and looking down at the garden, the cold breeze feeling good against her heated body clad in only a thin nightshirt which stopped at mid-thigh. She wanted to dance and sing.

"What do you suggest?" Let her take a call as he didn't want to offend her by offering a brief fling.

"Let's take it a step at a time. Brunch tomorrow and then…"

"Dinner again?"

If she had her way, she would have him for brunch. Grimacing, she replied, "Not tomorrow. I have to go for a *sangeet* ceremony."

"And I am at my cousin's wedding the whole of Sunday." He groaned.

She could feel him. "If it's any consolation, I also have to go to a wedding on Sunday."

"As you say, let's first meet for brunch. I'll pick you up whenever you say. Ping me."

"Hmm." She was reluctant to disconnect the call. "Arjun…"

"Hmm…"

"I don't know anything about you, I mean your personal life."

"There's not much to know. What I would like is to know all about you."

Kiara pouted. He obviously didn't want to share anything about his personal life. Or maybe it was too soon. "I thought my life must be an open book to you by now." A sudden yawn took her unawares, making her sound funny.

"Hahaha! You are sleepy. Good night then. I'll see you tomorrow."

"Mwah." Kiara blew him a kiss before disconnecting the phone and falling into her bed, not aware she had only made Arjun all the more awake with the kiss she blew him over the phone.

Arjun glared at his phone, dropping it on the side table before getting up to dress. He might as well go for a run as sleep was nowhere in the vicinity.

18

Kirit invited Harish to go along with him to meet his lawyer, Prakash Shinde. The lawyer was even more crooked than Kirit and they suited each other very well.

"*Kaise ho*, Prakash *Bhai*?" Kirit greeted the lawyer on entering his office cabin.

"I'm fine, Kirit*ji*. Welcome, welcome. You should have phoned me and I'd have rushed over even if it was short notice." Prakash gave his rich client a wide grin, showing off all his *paan*-stained teeth.

Oh yes, and you would have charged me double, thought Kirit as he sat down in one of the chairs in front of the lawyer's work table, pulling Harish down to sit next to him.

"*Ladka kaun hai*?" asked Prakash, eyeing the younger man.

"Harish is my nephew. He's working for me nowadays." Kirit didn't let on he had been chucked out of his money-minting financial director's job with the Mathur Group of Industries. He was only too aware of the shark Prakash Shinde was.

"Oh really! That must be nice. Hello, Harish. Nice to meet you. Do you like your job?" asked Prakash, beckoning to the office boy who had pushed opened the door. "Bring three cups of tea," he instructed the boy on an aside before turning his attention back to his clients.

Harish shrugged. "I like working with my uncle," he said in a small voice. The truth was he didn't like it at all. His uncle treated him like a servant, making him carry his briefcase, fetch coffee and tea, go out to buy cigarettes and *paan* for him. It was not a job really. He had been better off at the furniture company. Then, he could at least claim to have a proper marketing job. With his uncle, he was a cross between an office peon and a house servant. But there was that promise his uncle had made, to make Harish his *waaris*. Harish lived in hope.

"If I were to resign my post as financial director… just a thought, mind you." Kirit looked at Prakash to gauge his reaction as he uttered the words, while sipping from his cup of tea.

"Hmm." Prakash wanted to hear his client out fully before giving his opinion.

"I own half a per cent of the company's shares, which is worth four crore rupees in today's market. The value's only going to increase as time goes on." Kirit continued to wax lyrical about the Mathur Group of Industries, not missing the fact that Harish was even more impressed than the lawyer, his jaw hanging wide open as he stared at his uncle in awe. Good! It was best to keep the lad hooked to the idea of becoming his heir. "What I want to know from you, Prakash *Bhai*, is this: what are my powers in such a case? I will still be on the board, you understand?"

Prakash nodded, his thoughts racing. Why would Kirit want to give up his post as financial director? "Do you have a copy of the articles of association of your company?" he asked.

"I can have a copy delivered to you. How will that help?"

"I'll be able to tell you where you stand after I read it," said Prakash, drinking from his teacup.

"*Haan*. And I want you to create a document for my Will."

Why now? Prakash couldn't help wondering. He had been advising Kirit to document his Will from the day he had become his client. Which had been five years ago. But he didn't ask the question, only nodding in agreement. "Do you want to discuss the features of your Will now?" He gave Harish a pointed look, trying to draw Kirit's attention to his nephew. Generally, a Will was made without the knowledge of people, especially members of one's family.

"Of course, now. I want to leave everything to my nephew Harish here." He gave an extra loud laugh. "Of course, it will be his responsibility to take care of my wife if I pass on before her. I'm sure he will do that, won't you, Harish?"

Harish couldn't believe his ears. Kirit Uncle had promised to make him his *waaris*. This was the first he had heard about the four crore rupees worth of shares which his uncle owned. There was his house—

an apartment in Andheri West—and he must be having cash in his bank as well. Did that mean Harish was going to be the sole heir to all of this? He was spellbound by the turn of his luck. It didn't strike him that Kirit was not even sixty years old and might live to be eighty or more. And until then, Harish might have to continue with his servile existence. Just now, he turned to his uncle with a sheen of tears in his eyes. "Yes, Uncle. I'll take care of Asha Aunty for you."

"There! Everything is settled." Kirit rubbed both his hands together gleefully. "You draw the Will, Prakash *Bhai*, and I will sign it. Can we have it ready by the end of this week?"

Prakash looked from one man to the other, wondering what was going on. Kirit wasn't playing to his character. If he knew the man—and Prakash was an expert at studying characters and had never failed in all these years—he was making a complete fool of his nephew; probably setting him up as a fall guy. Something was definitely amiss here.

"But, of course, Kirit*ji*. Let me do something. I'll make a list of all your assets from the information I already have from your accountant. You please verify the list for me before I draw your Will. Shall I mail the same to you by end of day tomorrow?"

"Perfect!" approved Kirit, getting up to his feet. "You are my man, Prakash *Bhai*. I'll wait for your email. In the meanwhile, have a good day." Taking Harish by the hand, Kirit exited his lawyer's office, a bounce in his step.

rjun went to Kiara's house to pick her up at 10.30 am. She rushed out of the gate to meet him outside, not keen on her mother seeing him. Kalpana was capable of making marriage plans immediately.

"Good morning, Arjun."

"Good morning, Kiara."

She was a sight to behold. Wearing a pair of dungaree shorts in black velvet corduroy, teamed with a peach-coloured t-shirt, Kiara looked so young and beautiful, like a breath of fresh air. She had tied back her hair with a piece of silk ribbon, her face free of make-up except for a touch of peach gloss on her wide lips. Her feet were encased in sneakers the same shade of peach as her t-shirt, leaving her long, long legs bare.

Leisurely running his gaze from the top of her head to the soles of her feet, Arjun gave a soft whistle, making colour bloom on her cheeks. "You look lovely."

Kiara gave him a bright smile even as she studied him. In a pair of dark blue designer jeans and a long sleeved, slim fit t-shirt in jet black, he looked stunning. His body was honed to whipcord perfection, the absence of a collar drawing her gaze to the strong muscles of his throat. "And you look hot," she retorted, thrilled to see the ruddy colour rush up his lean cheeks.

It was only as he was opening the car door did Kiara notice the two-seater Mazda MX-5 Miata in a brilliant shade of red. "Whoa!"

"You like it?"

"It's adorable. Does the top open up?"

He reached across her to press a button and the top slid back to let the sun shine down on the black leather seats. "Do you want to drive?" he asked.

Do I? Just now she wanted to focus her attention fully on the hunk next to her. "Let me watch you drive and maybe later."

Settling into the driver's seat, he nodded. "How hungry are you?"

"A bit. Can hold for an hour maybe."

"Tangerine Café at The Retreat Hotel offers an excellent buffet lunch. The best part is it's never too crowded, even on Saturdays. I thought we can take a long ride to Madh Island and then go there for lunch. If you're hungry, we can have a bite somewhere along the way. Do you like street food?" He turned to glance at her as he navigated through the morning traffic.

"I can binge on street food, any damn thing. You?"

He smiled. "Like any other Mumbaikar, I also love *vada pav* and *chaat*."

She snapped her fingers. "Let's have *vada pav* and *ganna ras*."

He nodded, giving her an indulgent smile. She looked so young she could pass off for a college student. Sitting next to her Arjun felt so old and jaded. "Perfect. Let's go." When the car picked up speed, her curls took wing. It wasn't long before the silk ribbon flew away, letting her hair completely free. When she turned towards him, the curls blew across her face, making her laugh, fascinating the man at the wheel no end.

She switched on the car radio and tuned it to her favourite FM channel, humming along with a popular Bollywood song.

Arjun felt peace steal over him, making him completely relax for the first time in years, bringing a soft smile to his face. He stopped the car at the beach and parked at a pay-and-park, after placing the hood back.

Kiara removed her shoes. "Let's walk along the beach."

He shrugged, removing his shoes and socks before rolling his jeans up to mid-calf. Taking her hand in his, he walked towards the water. "After a bite of breakfast, I think. I'm famished."

They walked to a vendor who was making fresh *batata vada*. Arjun asked for two *vada pavs*. A woman helped the vendor by quickly spreading green chutney inside two *pavs*, before dusting them with the red *lasoon chutney*. Watching her action, Kiara smacked her lips. "I am sure it'll taste divine."

Arjun couldn't help smiling when he saw her eager face as she eyed the snack. He received the piping hot *vadas* enclosed in the *pavs*, before handing one over to her. He watched, captivated, as Kiara took bites of the snack, her small pearly white teeth sinking into it time and again.

"Aren't you eating?" she asked, looking up at the man who was staring at her.

He gave a nod before biting into his *vada pav*. It was absolutely delicious. "Would you like one more?" he asked her.

Kiara shook her head vigorously. "Don't tempt me. This will be more than enough till lunch time."

"Tea or sugarcane juice?" he asked.

"Tea, I think," she responded immediately.

He turned to the vendor and said, *"Do chai bhi dena."*

Arjun took the two glasses of tea the man at the cart handed him, passing one to Kiara. He smiled when she blew at the tea before sipping from the glass.

Kiara lifted an eyebrow at him. "Is something funny?" she asked.

He shook his head. "Not funny. Just that you look so cute when you blow at the tea to cool it, just like a kid."

She grinned. "If that makes me appear like a kid, then I'm going to be a kid forever," she declared.

Arjun stared at her, startled by her answer. It seemed like a truly innovative way of looking at life.

By mutual consent, they stepped over to the water's edge and began to walk along the beach.

Arjun recalled the time when he had been maybe nine or ten. He had walked on the same beach with his parents on both sides, holding their hands as he skipped along the water's edge.

The memory rolled by to be replaced by another. The time when he had spent here with Mudit and a few other friends. He had been seventeen then. They had brought a dozen bottles of beer and had drunk their way through the lot, hanging out at the beach until sunrise.

After that…

…this was the first time he had stepped on a beach after that. It had been thirteen years, maybe a little longer.

Kiara hugged his arm, pressing close to his body invitingly. Just then a huge wave came by, making them race up the shore. She burst out laughing, enjoying the spray thrown up by the wave.

Arjun turned to look at her, a smile tugging at his lips. Cuteness overload! That's what she was. Of its own volition, his left arm went around her shoulders as he hugged her close.

"Arjun?" Kiara looked up into his eyes. It was a good thing he was facing the sun while she, in the opposite direction. His eyes shone in the bright light of day, the pupils narrowed, surrounded by honey brown irises which made her want to drown in them.

"Hmm." His eyes roamed over her face, stopping at her luscious lips. Bending his head, he kissed one corner of her mouth, just the way she had done the previous night. Only, he didn't stop with it. Or rather, his tongue seemed to have a mind of its own as it peeped out to trace the seam of her lips.

Kiara shuddered with longing as she felt the tip of his tongue exploring the shape of her mouth. Her hands on his chest, she stepped on his feet to press her mouth to his even as his arms came around her waist, pulling her close to his taut frame.

And he kissed her as if his whole life depended on it, his teeth nibbling her lips even as his tongue demanded entry into her mouth.

Kiara opened her mouth to suck on his tongue, pressing her own against his.

With a moan, Arjun tightened his arms around her slim waist as he kissed her deeply, his tongue clashing with hers.

The next wave almost brought them to their knees, forcing them to break the kiss abruptly. Kiara looked at him, laughing, her arms around his neck as she clung to him. "That's the best kiss I've ever had."

"Do you have a lot of experience?" he asked casually; too casually. He still didn't know what kind of a relationship she shared with Mudit.

"One, two. That's it!" She counted on the fingers of her left hand. "The first time Vinay kissed me, I wanted to throw up and that was the end of our relationship spanning all of three days."

"What?" A startled Arjun stared at her, wondering if she was serious or was simply making fun.

Kiara nodded. "Yep. It was so horrible that I don't even want to think about it. And the second one… we had sex but Suman wasn't into French kissing." She wrinkled her nose at Arjun as she spoke. "When I tried to kiss him, he ran away from me."

Arjun laughed out loud, totally enamoured by her frankness.

"And yes," she continued, "there was Harish. He was the first boyfriend I went out with. I was barely seventeen then." She scrunched up her nose once again. "He dumped me the moment I told him my dad's bank account had been wiped clean. Looked like he was after my money and not me, after all.

Arjun's face lost colour when he listened to her words. "Ouch! Were you terribly upset?"

"Upset?" Kiara looked up into his eyes, shrugging. "Maybe for about two minutes. It just shows the shallowness of what I felt for him. But then, he called my father a fool. It was a good thing he said so over the phone. Or he might have been slapped hard for his efforts. Idiot!"

Arjun smiled when he heard the temper in her voice. "So, do you have a boyfriend nowadays?"

She shook her head, her curls bouncing all over, some of them clinging to his arm. "Nope."

"Mudit?"

"What about Mudit?"

"You are friendly with him." Too friendly in Arjun's opinion. He was green with jealousy.

"We are definitely friends. He's like an elder brother to me and treats me like a kid sister. I don't have siblings and it was amazing growing up with him as my neighbour. I used to fight with him a lot when I was small. I even bit him once."

"Ouch!" Arjun was smiling now, the pressure on his heart lifted when he realised his friend wasn't seeing Kiara. "Poor Mudit!"

"Poor Mudit my ass!" Kiara stepped away from him, her fists on her slender hips as she made her point. "He laughed when I fell off a tree branch."

Arjun guffawed, surprising himself. "How old were you?"

"A little more than three. And he must have been six, I think."

Grinning, Arjun threw his arm around her shoulders once again as they continued to walk.

It was a while before Kiara spoke. "What about you? Any girlfriend?" she asked.

Arjun's face darkened as he removed his arm from around her. "No, I don't have one."

"Any ex-girlfriend?"

"I think we should go for lunch. It's past one." He didn't look in her direction as he walked swiftly back the way they had come.

Kiara realised he had clammed up once again and no amount of questioning was going to get her an answer. She decided to catch hold of Mudit and learn more about Arjun's personal life.

They got a corner table at the restaurant, overlooking the pool. They had a mild cocktail before tucking into the buffet lunch. But the magic they had shared at the beach had disappeared.

Kiara couldn't help wondering how long it would be before Arjun could be coaxed back into being cheerful.

Sigh! But she was determined that way.

That evening, wearing a *ghagra choli* in pastel green trimmed with sequins and gold thread, Kiara walked into the hall where her friend Dinesh's *sangeet* ceremony was to begin. While he had asked her to go for the dance practices over the last few weeks, she had simply not had the time.

Someone tapped her on her shoulder. Turning, her eyes went wide in surprise on seeing Mudit. "Hey, how come? You know Dinesh?"

Mudit grinned at her, shaking his head. "I know Dinesh's *fiancée*, Ritu. You know the one Arjun and I were speaking about at lunch the other day? Ritu is Arjun's cousin."

Kiara's heart dropped all the way down to her abdomen before raising up to clog her throat. Was Arjun here? He hadn't mentioned anything earlier, during their brunch date. A hand at her throat, she asked, "Is he here too?"

"No. He refused to come."

"He did? Why?"

Mudit shrugged. "He avoids most social occasions."

Kiara pouted. She wished she had known. She would have definitely dragged him to the function, or at least she would have tried to.

"And, by the way, you look nice." Mudit complimented her.

"You also look smart," she said, looking at his silk kurta of dull gold and the cream churidar.

"Thanks, ma'am, you made my day."

Kiara slapped his arm, laughing as they went to meet the bride and groom who were surrounded by a number of young friends and relatives.

Soon, the dances began in full swing, the item numbers which had been practised for taking precedence. After an hour and ten song and dances in which both Ritu and Dinesh participated with enthusiasm, a DJ took over and played songs for everyone to dance.

"Come," said Mudit, taking Kiara's hand in his and dragging her to the dance floor.

Kiara had the time of her life as they swung to the beats, laughing away. Mudit was a fun person to be with. But it was Arjun's company which she craved.

The bride's mother, Smita, tapped her sister Nandita on the shoulder. "Who is that girl dancing with our Mudit?"

Nandita lifted her head to look in the direction Smita was pointing at with the corner of her eyes. "Are you talking about the slim young girl in the light green *ghagra*?"

"Yes, that's the one. She has been clinging to Mudit from the moment she entered the hall. *Kya chakkar chal raha hai* between them I wonder?"

Nandita pulled a face, shrugging. "Our Mudit is a nice boy. Looks like the girl is very *chaalu*. After all, he's so rich. All single girls must be flocking to him like bees to a honey pot."

Though Mudit was related to them by neither blood nor marriage, the two older women felt it was their duty to protect him, all because he was Ritu's schoolmate and they had known him since he was a small boy. "I don't think she's Ritu's friend," declared Smita.

"Of course not. Our daughter is too sweet. This girl is obviously from Dinesh's side." Nandita turned to look at her sister. "Do you think she must have tried flirting with Dinesh as well?"

"*Che!* How horrible is that! What kind of parents would let their daughter go wild like this? Flirting with every man who comes her way?" Smita scowled, forgetting to smile at her own daughter's *sangeet*.

And all this long Kiara had only been dancing with Mudit, not even touching him. But somehow, Ritu's mother and aunt had concluded she must be a flirt, all because she was attractive, probably more beautiful than most of the young women who were at the *sangeet* that evening.

Kiara lifted a hand and called a halt, laughing breathlessly when a slow number began. "I need a break. Let's go have something to drink, Mudit. I'm parched."

"You've grown old, Kiara, my dear," teased Mudit, "we've been dancing for less than an hour and you're already beat."

"Beat! It's you I'm going to beat, Mr Trivedi. I just want a short break and a drink before hitting the floor again. Anyway, dancing to slow numbers is just not me."

He grinned, taking her elbow in his as they walked towards the bar which had been set up at one end of the hall. "Beer for you?"

Kiara shook her head. "I'll have a lemonade."

"Why?" he asked in a dramatic whisper, "you've stopped drinking or what?"

She pouted at him, saying, "Just for today."

"Why? What's special about today?" Mudit persisted as he placed an order for a lemonade for her and a whiskey and soda for himself.

"*Tum bhi na*, Mudit."

Mudit grinned mischievously. "What did I do?"

She took the lemonade from the bartender and walked away from Mudit to one corner of the room.

A laughing Mudit followed right after her once he picked up his drink from the counter. "Want to eat something?" he asked.

Kiara wrinkled her nose up at him. "Later maybe."

"What's up? You seem…" he paused to study her face with his deep grey eyes before continuing, "you seem disturbed about something." This was probably one of those rare times. The Kiara he knew was a bundle of mischief who laughed at anything and everything.

"Promise me something first." Kiara placed her empty glass on the window sill before speaking to her best friend in earnest.

"Eh? You sound serious."

"I am. Promise me."

"What am I promising here?" he asked, the laughter disappearing from his face as he stared at her. "Don't freak me out, Kiara."

"I'm going to let you in on a secret. Don't you dare mention it to anyone."

Mudit placed a hand over his heart and said solemnly, "I promise. Go on, tell me."

"I'm in love with Arjun."

Mudit guffawed and guffawed some more, until he felt a small fist attack his shoulder. "Ouch!" he groaned dramatically.

"Just be happy we are in public or otherwise it would have been my foot to your solar plexus," snarled Kiara, glaring at him.

"But… but why?"

"Why what, you idiot?"

"Why do you want to beat me up?"

"Why did you laugh at me when I said what I did?" A film of tears formed over Kiara's eyes as she continued to glare at him. "And here I thought you were my best friend. I…"

"Hey! Kiara." Mudit hugged her. "I'm sorry. I shouldn't have laughed. It's just that…"

"Just that what?" She sniffed.

Mudit shook his head. "I'm really sorry. First of all, I've always thought of you as my buddy. You know, my friend, someone I hang out with. There are times I forget you are a woman. I…"

Kiara moved away, her bunched fists on her hips as she gave him an accusing look, her dark eyes appearing dangerous.

Mudit lifted his hands in front of him in a gesture of defence. "Come on, Kiara. You exactly know what I mean."

"You think it's funny I fell for a guy and not a girl? Is that what you mean?"

He shook his head vigorously. "*Arre yaar*, don't put words into my mouth. Okay, let me apologise once again. I'm sorry I laughed. It's just that you are so bubbly and Arjun is so bloody serious. I kind of… I'm amazed is all I can say."

A soft smile lit up Kiara's face as her thoughts revolved around Arjun. "What they say about opposites attract, it must all be true I suppose."

"Who are "they"?" Mudit drew quotation marks in the air, his eyes dancing with mischief once again.

"Mudit Trivedi! Get out of my life." Kiara's voice had risen by several decibels by now, uncaring there were people around them.

"Is everything alright?" asked Ritu, her eyes curious as she walked over with her *fiancé*.

Mudit threw an arm around Kiara's shoulders and said, "Of course, Ritu. Swell party, I must say."

"But Kiara doesn't seem happy," said Dinesh as he stood next to Ritu, his arm around her waist.

Kiara shook her head. "The party is amazing, Dinesh."

"But something has upset you."

She grinned. "Of course not. I was just bickering with Mudit, nothing serious."

"Oh, okay. The dance floor is awaiting you guys. Come along!"

It was much later at night when they got into a cab before Mudit asked, "So, tell me. Did you mean it back there when you told me about falling in love with Arjun?" His voice was serious for a change.

Kiara nodded. "Yes."

"Does he know?"

She shook her head. "Of course, he doesn't. He's not someone I can walk up to and declare, 'I love you' to. You should know that much about him."

Mudit was nodding even before she completed the sentence. "Exactly." There was a worried frown on his face. "He doesn't like women. Wait a minute, that came out all wrong. I am not suggesting he's queer. It's just that he dislikes women, intensely."

"Are you sure?" Kiara's eyes danced.

"Why? Do you know better?"

"He has been a little more than friendly with me for a guy who doesn't like women. Unless he also looks on me as a "buddy". You know, I could be either a guy or a gal for him to care."

"Don't be an idiot, Kiara. You and I go back a long way. Arjun cannot perceive you for anything other than a damn attractive woman."

"Well, thanks." Kiara was half sarcastic as she pouted at him.

"I'm serious. As for Arjun…"

"What about Arjun? Which is exactly what I want to know. I've been asking you about him, but you've not been very forthcoming."

Mudit sighed. "I only know he doesn't like women. But I don't know the reason for it."

"And you call yourself his friend."

Mudit shook his head. "Come on, Kiara. What's the connection? Of course, I'm his friend. But…"

"If that's true, you should know what his problem is. There's a deep sadness, you know, lurking right there at the back of his eyes. He doesn't even smile naturally. Don't tell me you haven't noticed."

Mudit was well aware of whatever Kiara said about Arjun. "Listen Kiara. I'm his friend, but that doesn't mean I'm privy to everything in his life."

"Which is what I don't understand. Why?"

"*Arre*! Guys don't gossip." Mudit was glaring at her by now.

"Gossip! Don't be an idiot, Mudit. Knowing what has upset your friend is not gossiping. Something or someone has hurt him badly. And he's still suffering." Kiara's voice turned hoarse as she dwelled upon Arjun's pain.

"But that's his business. It's too personal to him. How can I ask him about it?" Mudit was truly flummoxed.

"You are aware he's suffering, right?"

"Er… suffering is too strong a word. I know something has affected him, some incident from his past. But it's none of my business. I would never step into his space. And as his friend, that's what Arjun would expect of me," Mudit said firmly.

Kiara snorted. "I suppose it's a guy thing."

"Exactly what I've been trying to tell you."

"Okay, let me find out for myself."

"I know one thing about him. To be truthful, it's all hearsay, nothing I heard from the man himself," said Mudit, a warning note in his voice.

"What is it?" she asked.

"There was a woman during his university days. A foreigner, a Scot, I think. He was in love with her. But she died in an accident."

"I remember about that. You told me about the girlfriend who died in a car accident the other day." The smile disappeared from Kiara's face. "He must have been heartbroken."

"Probably still is."

"Don't tell me. How long has it been? Ten years or more maybe?"

Mudit shrugged. "About that long."

How am I going to compete with a ghost? Kiara was shaken, but not broken. With a determined thrust to her chin, she decided to simply go after what she wanted. Anyway, the other woman didn't exist anymore. How long could Arjun pine for her?

"Are you sure you are in love with him? And it's not just infatuation or maybe even lust?" Mudit sounded sort of worried. He didn't want Kiara to get hurt. Nor did he want Arjun to be hurt for that matter, not again.

Kiara gave her friend a brilliant smile. "It's all of that and more is what I feel for Arjun."

Overcome by emotion, Mudit simply hugged her.

"I didn't mention it before, but we both have been meeting, maybe you can call it dating. I went out for dinner with him last night and then for brunch today."

"Eh?" Mudit was surprised. He knew only too well how impulsive Kiara was. But it was so unlike Arjun to take a woman out, especially twice in the span of twenty-four hours. "Are we talking about the same guy? Arjun Mathur?"

Kiara grinned, thrilled to see the astonishment on Mudit's face. It just showed that Arjun's behaviour was something out of the ordinary.

They had spent more than four hours together that morning. Though Arjun didn't speak all that much, Kiara so enjoyed hanging out with him. And she had been enthralled by his melting brown eyes which simmered with heat whenever he looked at her.

"He's busy tomorrow, he said, attending a wedding. Hey, wait a minute! Could he have been talking about Ritu-Dinesh's wedding?"

Mudit laughed. "Bullseye."

Her excitement knew no bounds. After all, it would be the first time she would be meeting Arjun during a social occasion. Talk about getting dressed to kill! She was going to do exactly that for tomorrow.

Lost in her own world, Kiara gave Mudit an absent-minded wave when she got out of the cab to go into her house.

S mita had to hold back her frown with immense difficulty when Anjali handed over a gift cover to her. Why couldn't have Arjun given it to her or even to her husband Rana for that matter?

Their deceased brother's wife wasn't someone Smita or Nandita truly liked. At least not nowadays. It hadn't been like this in the beginning. When Jayant married Anjali and brought her home—it had been an arranged match, of course—both his sisters had accepted his nineteen-year-old bride as a younger sister. The three women had got along like a house on fire.

It was later, when Jayant had set up a house of his own did his sisters begin to blame Anjali for the decision. Having no clue to their own brother's bossy nature; about how he took decisions without ever bothering to consult his wife, they placed the blame entirely on Anjali's head. This was for Jayant shifting out of his parents' house and setting up his own home at Hiranandani Gardens. It never struck either sister that Anjali was but a doormat to Jayant. As their love for their younger brother was totally blind, they had concluded it was Anjali who had been the cause for breaking up the joint family.

Till date, they had been unable to forgive Anjali for no fault of hers. Nor had they ever sought to clarify the matter, either with their brother or with their sister-in-law. Later, when Jayant was murdered, it had been Anjali's fault. After all this, they had only gone on to hate her all the more when Anjali remarried. How could she even think of getting married to another man after leading such a wonderful life with Jayant for twenty years? Neither Smita nor Nandita could understand this. Left to their devices, they would have never spoken to Anjali after her second marriage, ever; not in this lifetime.

But there was Arjun, the nephew they adored. And even more importantly, they loved his money. After all, wasn't it the wealth their brother had earned and bequeathed to his son? Didn't they have a right to it? That Arjun had multiplied the fortune ten times over didn't strike them. All they wanted was for their nephew to share his wealth with his cousins—Smita's daughter Ritu and Nandita's son Rohan.

Arjun, for all his cynicism and anger towards the world in general, had been extremely generous, contributing towards Rohan's education abroad and now Ritu's grand wedding at a suburban 5-star hotel. In return, all he demanded was that his mother and stepfather should be treated with respect.

And there lay the issue! Smita and Nandita simply hated Anjali. As far as they were concerned, she was dead and buried along with their brother.

Just now, it was next to impossible for Smita to accept the gift—a cheque for ten lakh rupees—which Anjali had just given her. But then, how could she say no to the money?

"Congratulations Smita. I can see that all the arrangements have been carried out so beautifully." Anjali smiled at her ex-husband's sister.

"Thank you," said Smita, the smile not reflecting in her eyes. "Hasn't Arjun come?"

"Of course, he has. Parth and he said they will park the car and come over." Anjali could feel the powerful vibes of the other woman's dislike. But she didn't really care. She presumed Jayant's sisters blamed her for his death. Since Anjali felt no guilt regarding the matter, she couldn't care less. And of course, they didn't like the idea she had married a second time, that too, to someone as handsome and dashing as Parth. They felt it was the ultimate betrayal to their brother's memory.

Jayant's memory, my foot! Anjali thought to herself. But for Parth entering her life at the right time, she would have gone stark, raving mad, living the life of Anjali Mathur.

"Where's Ritu? Is she still getting ready?"

Smita gulped. *What does Anjali plan to do? Visit Ritu in her room?* Smita didn't care for the idea. *Ritu is my daughter.* Why should she be friendly towards her *mami* who has betrayed her *mama's* memory?

"She should be down in the hall in five minutes or so. Did you have breakfast?"

"I will, when Arjun and Parth are here."

Smita grimaced, hating it whenever her sister-in-law mentioned Parth's name. She couldn't help remembering the author from the time Jayant was murdered. The man had taken over the Mathur household as if it was his own. How much Rana detested him!

"Yes, please do. Rana is calling. I'll see you around." Smita made good her escape.

A small smile curved Anjali's lips when she saw the plump Smita almost running away from her. Her smile turned wider when she saw Arjun and Parth entering the wedding hall. Both handsome and tall! Both so loving! How she adored the two men in her life! She lifted her hand in a wave.

They quickly walked over to her side. "All okay?" Arjun asked his mother.

She shrugged, a grin tugging at her lips. "As always."

Arjun gritted his teeth. "I would like to kick a few asses."

"I hope you aren't going to make a scene," said Parth mildly, lifting an eyebrow at the younger man.

"Of course not. Let's leave immediately after the wedding."

"I hope we are going to have breakfast and lunch," said Parth, mischief lighting up his silver gaze.

Both mother and son looked up at him, aghast. "Maybe only breakfast?" said Anjali.

Parth shrugged, grinning. "Whatever you guys decide. As for myself, I could comfortably hog all the food I want. After all, it's Arjun who's footing the bill."

Anjali laughed even as Arjun grinned. "I suppose you're right. But do you really want to spend such a long time in this caustic atmosphere?"

"It's only your aunts and Rana who hate us. Everyone else likes us and we like them as well. So, it's not all caustic. We are here already and might as well have a good time." Parth enjoyed watching people and he didn't get too many opportunities since he rarely socialised. He didn't want to miss a readymade situation such as this.

"You think so, Mom?" asked Arjun, turning to look at Anjali.

"Parth's right. We are here for Ritu's wedding and I suppose we can sit through it."

Arjun nodded. "Okay then. Let me look forward to the next few hours of boredom," he said half sarcastically, making them both laugh loudly.

Mudit came up to them and said, "Hello, Anjali Aunty," hugging her.

Anjali returned his affectionate hug with equal enthusiasm, replying, "Hello Mudit. Congratulations! I hear you are the new finance director of the Mathur Group."

"That's right, Aunty. Thank you," he grinned, before turning to Parth and shaking his hand. "How are you, Parth?"

"I'm all good, Mudit, my boy. And how have you been? Congrats, Finance Director!" Parth shook Mudit's hand heartily.

"I'm fine, Parth and thank you." Mudit gave the older man a warm smile. "When is your next book releasing?"

"It should be out in two months."

"I'm looking forward to it." Mudit turned around to hug Arjun. "Hey man!"

"Hey! Why don't we go have breakfast? It's going to be a while before Ritu comes down, I believe."

"In a minute," said Mudit, turning in the direction of the faraway washroom.

"Are you expecting someone?" asked Arjun.

"Yeah, soon… and here she is."

Arjun turned around to look in the direction Mudit was gazing and it was an effort to keep his mouth from falling open when he saw a sari-clad Kiara walking gracefully towards them. He had almost not recognised the girl he had taken out for brunch only the earlier day; the one who had been clad in dungaree shorts and t-shirt during the outing.

The vision who was walking towards them was wearing a turquoise blue silk linen sari with a gold border and a sleeveless blouse which left her slim arms bare. His eyes gone wide in wonder, Arjun continued to stare at her, not missing the chunky jewellery and dangling earrings which swung back and forth with every step she took. Her hair was piled at the top of her head, giving her a classic appearance even as the corkscrew curls which had escaped the knot danced at the sides of her face.

"Hello Arjun," greeted Kiara in a breathless voice when she reached them, her eyes drinking in his face and figure. He was dressed in the latest Indian fashion in a deep red *kurta* along with a black sleeveless jacket which was subtly embroidered in a matching shade of red. He wore a black *churidar* and leather *mojaris*. A sight worth drooling over!

"Hi Kiara! This is a surprise," said Arjun, taking her hand in his as he studied her beautifully made-up face. It was obvious, at least to him, that the colour on her cheeks were not due to artifice. Outlined with a dark brown eyeliner, her eyes appeared larger than ever, shining deeply black, the lashes thick and curling. Her lips were a deep pink, inviting him to explore. "Is Ritu a friend of yours?" *Please God! Let her not be related to Rana Uncle of all people.*

"Dinesh is my friend."

"Oh okay." *She seemed to have more men friends than women.* "This is my mother, Anjali Bhardwaj and this is Parth, my stepfather," he introduced. "Mom, Parth, this is Kiara Bakshi. She consults for my company."

If Kiara was disappointed at having been relegated to only the role of consultant, she didn't show it when she turned towards the couple. "Hello Aunty, lovely meeting you. Now I know where Arjun gets his handsome looks from," she grinned, speaking frankly as she always did.

While Anjali smiled at the vibrant young woman her son had introduced her to, neither Parth nor Mudit missed the colour rising on Arjun's cheeks.

Anjali opened her arms and pulled young Kiara into a warm hug, pressing her cheek to hers. "Hello, Kiara. Lovely meeting you too."

Kiara was touched by the older woman's warmth. Here was a friend indeed. She then turned to Parth and said, "Hello Uncle! Mudit tells me you are Paul Bainsbridge. Please tell me it's true."

Parth laughed out loud, taking her hand in his. "Mudit is right. I suppose you've read my books?"

"All of them, a few times over. I hope you'll be here in the evening. I'll bring my copies over to get them signed, if it's okay with you? Pretty please!"

Parth grinned. "While I'd love to sign them for you, I don't think we would be here in the evening, my dear."

When Kiara looked disappointed, Anjali said, "But Arjun must bring you home to us for lunch or dinner soon. You can get your books signed then. Arjun?"

Arjun sported a completely dazed look on his face. Things were moving too fast and totally out of his control. He realised he wanted Kiara to himself and didn't want to share her with anyone, at least not for a long time. Unable to refuse his mother, he said, "Why not?"

Hearing his unenthusiastic response, Kiara was thoroughly disappointed. Keeping a bright smile fixed on her face, she said, "That would be lovely, Aunty. Thank you so much."

"So, what do you consult about?" asked Parth as they moved in the direction of the tables laid out for breakfast.

Kiara's eyes danced. "It's top secret. But I'll tell you since you are related to Arjun. I'm a hacker, an ethical hacker," she told him in a dramatic whisper, turning around to look this way and that to ensure no one was listening.

"Whoa! That's fantastic. I'm curious to know more. I hope we can talk sometime in regard to researching for one of my books."

Kiara squealed in joy, stopping in her tracks, uncaring she was in the way of the other guests who were on their way to breakfast. "Don't tell me! I'd love to." As an afterthought she said, "I'd be honoured."

Anjali watched her struggle to be formal while in reality Kiara was a fun-loving spirit. It looked like the girl was exactly what the doctor had ordered for her son. The mother couldn't help hoping and dreaming of wedding bells not too far in the future.

ow that Kiara was around, Arjun didn't feel at all bored at Ritu's wedding. He patiently greeted a lot of relatives and friends, even managed to smile and say 'hello' to Rana. He couldn't stand Smita's husband who seemed to hate his mother more than everyone else.

His eyes sought Kiara every few minutes, lighting up with pleasure whenever they fell on her. "What?" she asked, giving him a soft smile when she found his eyes on her yet again.

His eyes lit up in response. "You seem to be extremely busy."

She shook her head, colour running up her cheeks. "Not really. It's just that Dinesh wanted me to check to the comfort of some of his guests."

"You carry on, then," he said, a look of disappointment on his face.

She shrugged. "I'm all done now."

"In that case, spend some time with me," he invited, patting the seat next to his.

Seeing his mother and stepfather weren't around, Kiara walked over and sat down near him, their arms touching.

"What's your plan after lunch?" he asked, bending close to her ear.

"Nothing, really."

"Would you like to go home with me, to my apartment?" he asked, his hands clenched into tight fists as he felt his blood heating up with her proximity. What he planned to do once they got to his home was anybody's guess as Arjun didn't know it himself.

"Er… what about your mother and stepfather?" Kiara's voice was breathless as she asked the question, her heart beating double time even as excitement thrummed through her whole body.

Arjun shook his head. "They live in Parth's apartment. I live alone."

On hearing his words, blood rushed through her veins, heating her up. Kiara felt the tips of her breasts tighten just at the thought of being alone with him. With a smile on her face, she responded in a choked voice, "I'd love to go with you in that case."

Arjun took her hand in his, pressing his palm to hers. "I can't wait." He spoke in a whisper before letting go of her hand even as hot colour rushed up her cheeks.

Not very far away, Nandita saw the two of them sitting next to each other, their heads tilted close. *What the hell was happening here?* Gnashing her teeth, she turned around in search of her sister. The wedding ceremony was already over and Smita was busy greeting the guests who had lined up to congratulate the newly married couple. Walking over to her elder sister, Nandita tapped Smita on her shoulder.

"What?" asked Smita, an eyebrow up in query when she noticed the temper sparking in Nandita's eyes.

Stepping close to her, Nandita spoke right into Smita's ear, "Remember that girl who was flirting with our Mudit all of yesterday?"

Smita nodded vigorously. "What about her?"

"You're never going to believe what I'm going to tell you." Nandita built up her story dramatically for the maximum impact she could garner.

Smita's eyes went wide as she took her younger sister's arm to drag her over to a corner where no one could hear them. "Tell me fast, Nandu. Don't keep me in suspense or my heart might simply fail."

"That girl is flirting with our Arjun. Don't turn fast in case they notice us. Can you see Arjun sitting to your right in the fifth row?"

Without heeding her sister's words, Smita lifted her head to look over Nandita's shoulder to check out the chairs filled with the wedding guests before her gaze landed on Arjun and the beautiful Kiara sitting right next to him. She gasped, not letting on she found the pair of them looking so perfect together. She would never admit to it, not in exchange for all the money in the world.

"How dare she?" Smita gritted her teeth hard, so much so her jaw ached. "Do you think she's found out Arjun is way richer than Mudit maybe?"

"I'm sure that must be it. The bitch!" Nandita was beyond furious. "I wish we had Anjali's ear. She's the only one Arjun will listen to."

"I wouldn't be too sure, Nandu. Arjun loves us both and will listen if one of us were to talk to him. I don't know about you, but I am definitely going to warn him, to beware of this girl who has no qualms about chasing every young and eligible man she comes across."

"You really think so?" Nandita wasn't too sure.

"I'll talk to him during the reception when things will be a little less hectic compared to now. I'll be off now. I can see Rana beckoning to me."

Nandita nodded. "You must go in that case. I'm going to keep a watch on the girl for a while longer. I am curious to know who all she's going to play around with."

"You do that and don't forget to keep me updated," was Smita's parting shot as she walked over to where her husband was standing next to a radiant Ritu.

"Parth, do you think Arjun is interested in Kiara?" Anjali's tone was hopeful as she asked her husband when she got a few moments alone with him. A number of fans had surrounded him when they got to know he was the face behind the pseudonym, Paul Bainsbridge.

Parth smiled down at his wife, his eyes roaming over her lovely face. "Maybe he is."

"Parth!" Anjali pouted at him. "What kind of an answer is that? Is he, or isn't he?"

"That question, my sweetheart, only Arjun can answer. Somehow, I think it's too soon to ask him. Why don't we wait and watch how it pans out?"

"Hmm!" Her sigh was long and expressive. "I suppose you're right." Only Anjali was too impatient to wait and watch. She knew for a fact Arjun had been heartbroken when Jane died. But holding a candle to a dead woman for eleven years was simply too much, especially considering he had known her for barely two years before that. While she had never said anything to her son regarding his single status, she was most definitely bothered about it.

Parth threw an arm around her shoulders and hugged her. "Do not worry, Anjali. It's the first time Arjun is showing interest in a woman after the Jane fiasco. We can live in hope, surely."

Anjali pulled out of his hug to face him, a small scowl on her face. "Fiasco? What do you mean by the Jane fiasco? Are you blaming her, all because she died in an accident which was no fault of hers?" She was surprised by her husband's words, actually. The Parth she knew was acutely sensitive to people and their feelings.

Parth realised his gaffe the moment Anjali pulled away from him. Shit! He had guarded Arjun's secret for eleven long years, but it had taken only a moment and one wrong word for Anjali to give him a suspicious look. "Let's talk when we get home." Maybe it was time for Anjali to know the truth. It wasn't as if she was a weak woman. But at that time, both Arjun and Parth had been clear not to share the truth with her. It hadn't been long after she recovered from her bout of depression and then Jayant's murder.

Anjali continued to frown up at her husband. *What does he know that I don't?* It wasn't at all like Parth to keep things from her. She trusted him, absolutely.

"Trust me, sweetheart," he said in a soft whisper, looking deeply into her honey brown gaze which held a disturbed expression in them.

The frown disappeared immediately from Anjali's forehead as she smiled at him, her hand on his arm as she pressed close to him. "Always, my Parth."

“I need a favour,” said Arjun to Mudit.

“Shoot!”

“Can you drop Mom and Parth back home?

Mudit hid the smile which sprang to his lips even as he nodded. “Come on, Arjun, it’s no big favour. Any time.”

“Thanks, Mudit. I owe you one,” said Arjun, a glimmer of a smile reflecting in his eyes as he spooned the last bite of *moong dal halwa* into his mouth.

“I presume Kiara doesn’t need a ride back home?” Mudit couldn’t help teasing his friend.

“How would I know? You’ll have to ask her that,” said Arjun, his face serious.

Just as a small frown formed on Mudit’s forehead, Kiara walked up to them and said, “Mudit, I’m leaving with Arjun. He’s promised to drop me home later,” making Mudit laugh out loud. “I don’t understand. Did I say something funny?” Kiara gave him a mock frown, her eyes dancing, her excitement palpable.

Mudit shook his head, still amused. “You go on, guys. I’ll catch you later in the evening.”

"I don't think we'll be coming for the reception," said Arjun firmly, turning to look at Kiara, his eyebrow raised in query.

"That's right, we won't be," she responded in a breathless voice, her hand tucked into Arjun's elbow.

"Mudit?" Arjun called to his friend who was looking at Kiara with a mischievous expression on his face.

"Yep!" Mudit turned to Arjun, unable to hide the amusement on his face.

"Can you deal with…?"

"Anjali Aunty and Parth? No worries there. I'll take care of them."

"I haven't told them I'm leaving. I…"

"What are friends for?" Mudit grinned, slapping Arjun's shoulder playfully. "You go on."

Arjun made a quick exit with Kiara on his arm. A valet brought his car around to the front and they left immediately after.

Once Mudit dropped them outside *Olympus*, Anjali gave Parth a wide grin. "I think Arjun is really interested in Kiara."

"Seems so," said Parth as they got into the elevator.

"Imagine dumping us and leaving with his girlfriend." Anjali laughed.

Parth grinned, happy for her as well as for Arjun. For the first time in years, he had seen Arjun smiling a happy smile, not the lip service he had got into the habit of offering everyone who walked within a few feet of him.

"So, are you going to tell me about the Jane fiasco?" asked Anjali when they entered their penthouse apartment on the thirty-fifth floor.

"I suppose it was too much to hope you had forgotten," said Parth, tongue-in-cheek.

"Parth!"

"Okay. Let me get some water to drink first." He got a bottle from the fridge and settled down on the sofa, Anjali on his lap. "What do you want to know?"

"Everything you haven't told me about Jane."

Parth gave a long sigh.

"How bad can it be?" asked Anjali, turning on his lap to look at him.

Parth grimaced. "Worse. Jane was driving a senior student's car when it crashed. She was running away with Peter to get married."

"Whattttt????" Anjali jumped off his lap to glare at him. "You are joking! Jane was in love with Arjun."

Parth shook his head slowly. "That's what Arjun had believed until the day of the fatal accident, when he found out she was in love with only his money, and never him."

"Oh my God! My poor baby!" Anjali was shocked to the core of her being. "Are you sure about it? She died on the spot, right? How do you know Peter was telling the truth? Maybe he was lying, just to be spiteful."

"I wish it were true." It looked like he had opened a can of worms. "But the truth is Jane was eloping with

Peter when she drove the car into an accident. She died while Peter lived to tell the tale."

Anjali was visibly pale when he dragged her back down on his lap, hugging her close. "I'm sorry to give you such a shock, sweetheart. I…"

"Why didn't either of you tell me anything then?" Even her son hadn't breathed a word to her.

Parth kissed her forehead. "You had enough on your plate then, Anjali. It hadn't been all that long since…"

"…I had recovered from depression. Tch! I've been a horrible mother."

"Eh?! Where did that come from?" He lifted her face up to his, a fist under her chin. "Come on, sweetheart! You aren't being fair to yourself."

"Arjun must have been terribly shaken."

"He was."

"He called you." Anjali's temper was on a slow boil. "Which is why you rushed to London, right? It wasn't your agent who called you, but Arjun." She recalled Parth's preoccupation when he left for the airport. She suddenly caught hold of the flaps of his jacket and shook him. Only he wouldn't budge, sitting there like a rock, his hands at her waist, waiting for the storm to blow over.

Parth gave a nod.

"And you still think I'm a good mother?" There was a sheen of tears in her big brown eyes.

"Of course, you are. Arjun will be the first one to agree with me on that."

"But he didn't bother to call me when he was in need. It was you he called."

"Does that mean I'm a great stepfather, better than his mother?" Parth shook his head at her, saying, "That's just crap and you know it."

Silent tears flowed down Anjali's cheeks. She felt guilty she hadn't been there for her son, all because the men in her life had believed her to be too weak to handle the issue at hand.

Picking up some tissues from a side table, Parth gently wiped her face, pulling her close to kiss her cheek. Could he escape not revealing the secret of Arjun's suicide attempt? Or should he make a clean breast of everything? He quickly concluded that it was best to get everything off his chest at one go.

"There's more to the issue, Anjali. And it's best you know about it."

Anjali lifted her face from his shoulder to look up at him. "What more can there be? Nothing worse than what you have told me already."

"Forgive me, sweetheart. There was a reason for Arjun contacting me and not you."

"Don't keep building up the suspense, Parth," said Anjali, irritated. "Tell me all at one go."

"He slashed his wrist when he found out Jane hadn't loved him at all, but only his money."

"What the hell are you saying?" Anjali was screaming now. She would have jumped off his lap once again, only Parth, with his arms tightly wrapped around her slim body, refused to let go.

"You heard me."

"Arjun tried to take his own life? Are you saying my son is a coward?" In contrast to her earlier words, her voice was a pathetic whisper now.

"Don't judge him, Anjali. He was heartbroken and acted impulsively. He…"

"But… but Arjun is, was, still is courageous. He's bold. He's running a multi-million-dollar empire. How could he attempt suicide?" Anjali was too upset for words.

"That's Arjun today. Then, he was a heart-broken twenty-year-old student, feeling completely betrayed."

"Could you forgive him so easily?" She sought her husband's assurance, searching his face.

Parth grimaced. "Not in the beginning. I blew my top, bit his head off actually. It was later that I…"

"What did you do later?" Anjali knew how much affection Parth had for her son. It was only today she realised how much he loved Arjun. A soft smile lit her face, like a ray of sunshine after a bout of heavy rain.

"I hugged him and consoled him. What else? He was a kid those days, Anjali. Please don't be angry with him." He brushed back the lock of hair which had fallen on her forehead.

Anjali actually grinned. "You are the best stepfather in the world, my Parth." She threw her arms around his neck and clung to him. "Thank you for being there for my son in his hour of need. I…"

"Oh… kay! That's where Arjun gets his vote-of-thanks habit from. Now I see."

"Huh!" She pulled away to look at her husband's face. "What are you talking about?"

Parth was shaking with laughter. "Are you even aware how you were thanking me formally just now?

Have you forgotten I'm your lover and husband who loves you more than anything else in the world?"

"So?" Anjali tried to glare at Parth's dear face, failing miserably.

"Why do you need to be so formal and thank me in so many words?" he asked, leaning forward to nuzzle her neck.

"How else do I show my gratitude?" she challenged him, "And I'm grateful you were there for Arjun in his hour of need, Parth. I'd have probably clobbered him for what he did and he just might have died anyway." Anjali could joke about the situation now.

"Hmm…" He traced a path with his tongue all the way from her neck to her mouth, pausing at the pulse points as he took his own sweet time. "I can think of a number of ways you can show me your gratitude. I…" He paused to take a deep breath before brushing his mouth gently across hers, again and again… and again.

Unable to bear the teasing, Anjali reached up to kiss him deeply, melting in his arms. "I love you, my Parth. I'm so lucky and so is Arjun, to have you in our lives."

"'nough said," he growled before lifting her up in his arms and carrying her to their bedroom.

Arjun pushed the inner door to his apartment open before turning to invite Kiara in, flinging his right arm out in a gesture of welcome.

Kiara stepped over the threshold, her dark eyes sweeping over the L-shaped hall even as her heels sunk into the deep pile carpet. When she saw Arjun removing his *mojaris* next to a shoe rack near the entrance, she immediately followed suit with obvious relief. Her stilettos weren't the best footwear for the long haul and she had been walking around in them from nine in the morning. It felt so good to be free of them finally.

"I'm going to get out of these clothes into something more comfortable. Would you like to change too? Maybe a t-shirt?" Arjun lifted a dark eyebrow in her direction even as his eyes ran over her slender figure clad in the lovely sari. While she looked gorgeous, he was sure she might prefer to change into something casual.

"Yes, please," said Kiara, giving him a broad smile. It had been wonderful dressing up for the wedding. But she had had enough of it by now.

"Have a seat and I'll be with you in a minute," said Arjun, walking further into the swanky and well-furnished apartment.

Kiara turned to her right and was glad when her eyes fell on the open kitchen. She swiftly walked over to find the fridge on the left. Opening it, she removed a water bottle and drank from it thirstily, parched after the heavy wedding lunch.

"Hey! You found water. I'm sorry I didn't offer you some."

She shrugged, offering the half-full bottle to him before taking the dark red t-shirt he had brought for her.

He finished the water before leaving the empty bottle next to the sink. Turning, he said, "Come with me," before guiding her to one of the two guest bedrooms to the left side of the main hall.

"I like your flat. It's so cosy," said Kiara.

He gave her a half smile. "I'm glad." Pointing to the first bedroom on the left, he said, "You can change in here. There's an adjoining bathroom. Feel free."

She gave him a nod and a smile before pushing open the door, stepping in and shutting it behind her. She was glad to notice the air-conditioner was already turned on, probably by remote. The room felt so fresh and cool. It was obvious no one used it. She wondered if Arjun had guests over often. After all, the apartment was kind of large for a single occupant.

Removing her jewellery, she placed them on the dressing table before quickly pulling off her sari. She folded it neatly, leaving it on the bed, soon following it with her silk petticoat. It was only when she removed the ties at the back of her blouse did Kiara remember it had an inbuilt bra. Which meant she had no spare one to wear under the t-shirt. Grimacing, she looked into the mirror, her eyes wide as they fell on her breasts. At size 34-C, they were a handful, firm and plump. Nice!

She went into the bathroom to thoroughly wash her face, neck, and shoulders to remove all her make-up, before freeing her corkscrew curls from the knot she had tamed them into. Using the hair brush she carried in her clutch, she brushed them vigorously until they fell around her face, shoulders, and mid-back in complete disarray.

Walking back into the room, Kiara pulled the t-shirt over her head, checking the shape of her breasts now, turning left and then right. It wasn't too bad. The t-shirt was thick and the shade of dark red camouflaged her shape well, or so it seemed to Kiara. The length of the garment wasn't bad either as it fell almost all the way to her knees. Pulling the sliding t-shirt over her left shoulder, Kiara stepped out of the guest bedroom into the hall, her eyes going immediately to the man seated on the sofa, his bare legs crossed at the ankles.

Sensing her presence, Arjun immediately got up and walked towards her, his gaze dropping down to check her bare legs, his mouth drying up at the sight. "Would you like to have something to drink?" he asked in a hoarse voice so unlike his baritone.

"Do you have green tea? I can make it."

He nodded, saying, "Allow me. Why don't you sit down and relax? I'll have it ready in a minute."

Kiara couldn't help but check his taut butt clothed in a pair of snug cotton shorts as Arjun walked towards the kitchen. *Boy! Was he drool worthy?!* She hoped he was going to make love to her.

Otherwise, she might simply have to take the initiative!

Arjun returned with two steaming mugs, offering her the one with a teabag before placing his black coffee on the centre table. Sitting next to her, he turned sideways, endlessly fascinated by her gorgeous hair. He reached out to pull at a curly strand, startled when it appeared to come to life as it twisted around his forefinger. Expecting it to be wiry and tough, he was even more amazed to find the thick strand so soft and silky. Leaning forward, Arjun drew the strand against his lips, totally enamoured. He appeared to be in a trance, not quite aware of what he was doing.

Her hand trembling, Kiara reached over to place her tea mug on the table, uncaring when some of the tea splashed over on the table. How was it even possible one could feel the sensation when someone touched the tip of one's hair? She had felt the tingle right up to her scalp, an electric current shooting all over her nerves when Arjun reached out to hold just one strand of her hair. Turning carefully, she looked at his face.

"Your hair is so incredibly soft," he said, his voice a gruff whisper, full of wonder.

Kiara shrugged, oblivious of the t-shirt sliding off her shoulder, drawing his gaze to the exposed curve of her right breast.

Arjun stared, unaware his hand had fisted over a bunch of curls as he watched his t-shirt slide slowly down Kiara's shoulder, baring her chest, a little at a time. He gave a shuddering sigh, a deep sense of disappointment when the t-shirt stopped sliding, exposing only the top of a creamy breast. "Kiara…"

"Arjun, you're hurting me," protested Kiara, reaching out to place a hand over his fist clutching her hair.

"What?" Arjun turned shocked eyes to his hand, even as he let go of her hair. "I'm so sorry, Kiara. I…" He got up immediately to walk to the window at the far end, his body rigid with tension. What the hell had he been doing? She was so soft and delicate; her hair so silky. How could he have been so rough on her? Arjun gripped the window rail hard, his knuckles turning white, his forehead pressed to the top.

"Arjun." Kiara got up to stand at his side, realising he had clammed up once again. She placed a hand on his back, only to feel his muscles tighten in protest. Without even fully realising what she was doing, Kiara lifted her hand to place it on his shoulder before running it caressingly down his back all the way to his waist. She continued to stroke his back at a leisurely pace, thrilled when she felt the tension leaving him, slowly but surely.

It wasn't long before he turned back to her. Gathering her in his arms, he buried his face in the crook of her neck, breathing deeply of her floral scent which was so unique to Kiara. How he wanted to make love to her!

Kiara hugged him, revelling in the hardness of his taut frame crushing her soft one. "Kiss me, Arjun," she invited, a wealth of desire in her voice which had gone hoarse.

Startled, Arjun lifted his head to look down at her. "Are you sure? I don't want to hurt you, Kiara. And it looks like I don't know myself. I seem to be violent."

She scowled up at him. "Violent? Whatever do you mean?"

His frown was way deeper than hers. "Maybe I don't know how to make love."

"You are joking."

He shook his head vigorously. "No, I'm not."

"Are you telling me you're a virgin?" Kiara's eyes were wide with shock.

A glimmering smile appeared on Arjun's face, chasing away his frown. It soon turned into a grin. "Don't be silly. Of course, I'm not."

"Well, then. What's the problem?" They were standing too close to each other for her to know for a fact that he wanted her, at least as much as she wanted him. She could feel his rigid shaft twitching against her abdomen.

"It's been really long since I've been with a woman," he confessed in a low voice, checking her face for reaction.

Kiara's face lit up with delight. "I'm glad it's me you want after all this long," she said, grinning right back at him.

Arjun shook his head, an amused expression on his face as he felt his heart lighten up. Kiara was definitely fun to be with. "Er… I'm not ready for commitment."

With a long sigh, Kiara shook her head at him. "Neither am I, Arjun," she said firmly. "But I want to make love with you, just now. Definitely this once. Let's leave alone any plans for the future. Please?" She lifted her face up to his, invitation in her eyes.

With a loud groan, Arjun bent down to capture her lips in a deep kiss, his arms tightening around her. It was a long time before they came up for air. "Will you tell me if I hurt you? I don't seem to be aware of my brute strength."

It seemed to Kiara he didn't know what being gentle was all about. With a wide smile on her face, she went on tiptoe to nip him on his chin, making him moan with longing. "A bit of hurting feels good. If it gets too much, I can always kick you in your groin. Works?" she asked, her eyebrows up as she playfully fluttered her eyelashes at him.

Looking deeply into her eyes to see if she was serious or was simply pulling his leg, Arjun noticed the flash of mischief and grinned at her, saying, "Perfect," as he lifted her up in his arms to carry her to his bedroom to the right side of the hall. Walking in, he deposited her on the bed. "You know, I like my t-shirt on you. Red suits you really well," he said, as he pulled his own t-shirt above his head.

Kiara stared at his bronzed and sculpted body as it emerged from behind the garment, her mouth wide open in wonder. He was gorgeous, with the body of a Greek God. She reached a hand to run it over his washboard abs. "You're perfect," she said in a loud whisper, looking up into his eyes.

Arjun caught her hand and held it against his abdomen, delighting in her touch. He couldn't help recalling that Jane had never touched him, not voluntarily. *Shit! Why the hell am I thinking of that scum?* A black frown gathered on his forehead.

"Is something wrong, Arjun? Don't you like me to touch you?" Kiara was on her feet as she stood in front of him, toe-to-toe. It was only too obvious he wanted her. But there was something bothering him, definitely. Some demon from the past. Was it the ghost of the girlfriend who had died in an accident?

"I like it only too much," he said, pulling her close to his chest.

"It doesn't seem so, not the way you are frowning," she responded, lifting a hand to run it over his forehead.

"Sorry, I got carried away with some morbid thoughts. I…"

Pulling her hands to herself, Kiara crossed her arms under her chest, looking up at him. "Does my touch bring forth morbid thoughts in you?" she challenged.

"Eh? Of course not."

"Of course, yes. I touched you and you frowned immediately." Kiara was not fighting with him, but only pointing out his reaction. She was keen to get any issue out of the way if they were going to make love any time today.

With a loud groan, Arjun sat down on the bed with a thud. "I don't know what to say, Kiara. I want you. But my mind… I…" he shook his head a couple of times before continuing, "I have a past. Nothing which you need to know. I…"

"Maybe you should talk about it, get it off your chest?" Kiara suggested gently.

He was already shaking his head before she completed her question. "I don't want to talk about it."

"Do you still want to make love with me?" she asked, placing a hand on his shoulder. She would kill him if his answer was in the negative.

Arjun lifted his face to hers in a flash. "Absolutely, yes. My body's been screaming for yours from the first time I met you," he said. To prove his point, he took her hand to place it against his crotch. "Do you believe me?"

Running her hand down his length, Kiara laughed gaily, long and loud, falling on his chest. "Arjun, you idiot! What are we waiting for?"

With an answering grin, Arjun removed the red t-shirt—his t-shirt—off her in a single sweep, his gaze avidly seeking her breasts, a long sigh ripping through him at the sight of her gorgeous twin globes. "You've an amazing body," he said, reaching a hand to cup her left breast, gently rubbing his thumb over the tip. He watched it pucker in response before he looked up into her eyes. "Kiara…"

Every nerve had come alive in her body, all of them ending right there at the tip of her left breast. She watched on, her gaze fascinated as she took in his hand holding her breast, so tenderly. She took his other hand and placed it on her right breast, breathing heavily when she felt his hold tighten on her. Her eyelids felt so heavy with languor as he kneaded her breasts in his large hands, tweaking the turgid nipples between his thumbs and forefingers.

"Are you going to sleep on me?" he asked, his lips on a shell-like ear as he reached out with his tongue to trace its shape.

"Hmm… mmm, no." Kiara turned her head a bit to accommodate his foraging mouth as he blew gently into her ear. Colour ran high on her cheeks as she felt the scrape of his chest hair on her sensitised breasts even as he pressed a hard cheek to her soft one.

"Your hair… I thought it's so curly and must also be prickly. But it's so soft," he said, running both his hands through the corkscrew curls, adoring the texture as he lifted a palmful and kissed it.

Kiara stroked her hands over his broad back, the muscles rippling under her touch. His back was as smooth as his chest was rough, she thought, revelling in the textures as she reached forward to kiss his shoulder, her small teeth nibbling him.

"I want to eat you up whole," he growled, his mouth on her slender shoulder as he gently bit into her skin, making her moan with longing. He traced his mouth from her shoulder bone, down the slope of her breast, taking small and gentle bites, making her writhe in pleasure. He teased her, running a damp tongue in circles around an aureole, round and round.

"Arjun!" She almost screamed with longing, desperate to have his mouth close over her taut nipple.

"What?" He lifted his head to look down at her, a smile in his gorgeous honey brown gaze. "Did you want something?"

"You know what." She gave him a mock glare.

He shook his head, an innocent expression on his face. "Nope. You tell me."

"I want your mouth on me," she groaned, "NOW!"

With a laugh, Arjun bent down to run his tongue over her breast tip, making her jump off the bed. He repeated the action, stroking her turgid nipple repeatedly before closing his mouth over her breast and suckling it gently.

Kiara's legs thrashed when she felt the wetness between her thighs, her hands holding his head close to her body. It was heaven to feel his mouth on her breasts as he turned his head to give an equal amount of attention to her right breast.

Arjun ran his hand up a silky thigh, reaching a finger at the apex to find her all wet and ready. He caressed her feminine mound even as he sucked on her breast, smiling when he felt her body thrumming in response.

Kiara protested when Arjun moved away from her to reach into the drawer at the side of his bed. "Don't go."

"I'm going nowhere, sweetheart," he said, removing a condom and rolling it over himself, "just getting some protection."

"Oh!" She looked at his length, her eyes wide. *How is he going to fit into me?*

"You okay?" asked Arjun, reaching out to plant a kiss on her lips.

"Huh? I think so." She was staring at his penis in fascination, the colour having disappeared from her face, her small teeth worrying her lip.

Sensing that she wasn't really okay, Arjun gathered her into his arms, running his hand over her head in a caress. "What's troubling you?" he asked, kissing her on her forehead.

She looked up into his eyes searchingly, wondering how to tell him. But then, being frank by nature, Kiara asked outright, "How the hell are you going to fit inside me?"

"Eh?" Arjun looked startled for a second before he burst out laughing. "Is that what's bothering you, my Kiara? That I might hurt you?"

She shook her head vigorously, her curls dancing around her naked shoulders, captivating him thoroughly. "I know you wouldn't hurt me. But what if I disappoint you? If I don't give you any pleasure?" She bit her lower lip, her eyes wide with longing as they looked into his.

"There's only one way to find out, right?" he asked, a soft smile on his face. She was simply adorable. "Kiara." He kissed her deeply, his hands on her legs as he pulled them around his waist. He probed her vagina gently with the tip of his penis before pushing in slowly, little by little, until finally he was deeply and completely buried inside her. "Did I hurt you?"

"Not at all," said Kiara enthusiastically, locking her legs at the small of his back, thrilled by the sensation when he moved inside her.

And it began, the dance as old as time, with Arjun withdrawing and thrusting right back into Kiara, building a crazy tempo which made them both quiver with pleasure even as sweat gathered on their foreheads. Kiara felt the build up from deep within her womb as little waves of rapture crashed one over the other to become bigger and bigger before they all came together to explode in one colossal wave which broke the shores and drowned her. Moaning in ecstasy, Kiara dragged her fingernails down his smooth back, shaken to the very core of her being.

Arjun continued to pound into her, his breath coming out in gasps, his body slick with perspiration as he bent down to take the tip of a plump breast into his mouth, suckling on it rhythmically, shuddering as the pleasure wave crashed over him this time round, making him groan long and loud before he fell at her side, exhausted and completely sated.

Kiara cuddled close to him, like a kitten, sighing when she felt his large hand closing over her breast, his palm grazing over the sensitised tip. "That was amazing," she declared, kissing him on his chest.

Arjun opened one eye to look at her, unable to stop smiling. It had been a revelation. It had been worth the wait of almost eleven years to meet the right woman to make love to. He wasn't really surprised to find himself stirring once again. "I'll be back," he said, getting up to go to the bathroom. He quickly got rid of the condom before cleaning himself. Taking a hot and wet towel in his hand, he walked back to the bed and gently cleaned Kiara, removing the traces of their lovemaking.

Kiara had been half asleep when she felt the warm towel on her thigh. Opening her eyes wide, she was astounded to feel the gentle strokes as Arjun cleaned her. *He was amazing or what?!* At that moment, her love for him multiplied manifold.

Seeing that she was awake, he dropped the towel over the side of the bed before lying next to her. "Are you okay?"

Taking his hand and placing it against her cheek, Kiara said, "Ne'er been better."

"You think your body can take another round?" he asked, giving her a wide smile.

She studied his dear face. Somehow, he appeared younger and more carefree. If that's what sex with her had done to him, then she would be thrilled to make love with him every day of the week. "There's only one way to find out, right?" she said, tongue-in-cheek as she repeated his words of earlier, her black eyes dancing with mischief. She reached over to touch his shaft and was thrilled to find it rock hard once again. "My, my! Aren't we ready, already?"

Ruddy colour washed over Arjun's lean cheeks as he lay back on the bed. The determined thrust to her small chin made it obvious she had some plan stored for him.

Kiara got up to go on her knees, her hands stroking his length from the root to the tip.

Arjun watched her with half closed eyes, as she pleasured him, her breasts bouncing every time she moved. He let her have her way with him for some time before pulling her down on him as he thrust into her with a groan of pleasure.

Kiara rode him, thrilled when she felt his hands on her breasts, squeezing and petting them. It wasn't long before an orgasm ripped through both of them simultaneously and she fell on him like a rag doll, completely spent.

They fell asleep, holding on to each other, only to wake up later in the evening and making love again. It looked like neither could have enough of the other.

Kiara cuddled against his chest, her cheek pressed to his heart, revelling in the steady beat. She ran a hand over his shoulder, stroking it leisurely down his arm.

His face buried into her silky curls, Arjun couldn't stop the smile stretching his lips as his manhood responded instantaneously to her caresses. Insatiable! That's how they were. Moving away, he pulled her up on the pillow, turning her on her back, his gaze roaming over her piquant face, stopping at the wide lips swollen from his kisses. Leaning forward, he drew his tongue over the seam of her lips. "I can't seem to have enough of you."

Opening her mouth to his, Kiara relished his kiss before saying, "Same here. I seem to crave your touch, all the time."

"Hmm..." He kissed the hard beating pulse at her throat before moving down to trace his tongue over the curve of her left breast, nipping the plump flesh, even as he caressed the right one in his palm, a thumb and forefinger playing with the turgid nipple. "Kiara..."

It was past midnight when Arjun dropped Kiara at her home. She was wearing his red t-shirt, the clothes she had worn to the wedding in a carry bag. Leaning down to kiss him on his mouth, she said, "Take care. Good night."

"You too," he said. "Now go before I carry you back to my flat."

"Don't tempt me," she challenged, not moving an inch as she stood next to his car.

"Kiara. Go. Now."

"Spoilsport!" She pouted at him before turning and walking to the door. Opening it with her key, she turned around to wave at him, blowing him a flying kiss.

Arjun caught the kiss and pressed his hand to his lips, giving her a wave before leaving, whistling a tune under his breath as he navigated through the empty roads. It had been the most amazing weekend he had had in so many years. He couldn't wait to meet Kiara again.

Kiara walked into her office and was pleasantly surprised to see a large bouquet of red roses lying in a fat, blue coloured pot of Jaipur ceramic. Overwhelmed, she dropped her backpack on the floor to rush across and bury her face in the fragrant flowers. Seeing a white card tucked amidst the flowers, she removed it to see the words, "Thank you" written in a bold scrawl.

Arjun! How she loved him!

Her phone pinged. It was a message from him. "Come over to my cabin." He obviously knew she had reached. With a smile on her face, Kiara went into the adjoining washroom to check her face in the mirror. While it was the same face she had seen on Friday, it appeared sort of different... her eyes wearing a knowing look. With a smile and a wink at her image, Kiara stepped out of her office to walk to Arjun's.

Giving a cursory knock, she opened the door to find Mudit sitting across from Arjun. "Good morning, guys," she called out cheerfully.

"Good morning, Kiara," they seemed to say in a chorus, both of them grinning widely at her. Mudit, with his usual mischievous smile and Arjun… Kiara was thrown by the adoring smile on his face, her heartbeat picking up pace.

"I was just leaving," said Mudit, getting up from his chair. The air had grown thick the moment Kiara stepped into the cabin and he wasn't going to play *kabab mein haddi.*

Neither of the others seemed aware when Mudit left Arjun's office, shutting the door quietly behind him.

"Come here." Arjun lifted a forefinger to beckon to her.

Kiara moved forward in a trance and fell into his lap when he pulled her into his arms. She lifted her face to his and was thrilled to bits when he kissed her thoroughly.

"Good morning!" he said, his voice hoarse with longing. "Did you sleep well?"

"Like a baby," she said, pressing her lips to his smoothly shaven cheek. "I miss the fuzz on your face."

"Eh?" He gave her a cocky grin when he caught her meaning. "Tonight, I promise."

Looping her arms around his neck, she asked, "Are we going to meet tonight?"

Arjun didn't bother to answer her as he was busy removing the buttons on her shirt before pushing the flaps to the sides. Bending down, he kissed the curve of her breasts peeping above her lacy bra.

"Arjun! What if someone comes in?" Kiara made a half protest.

"I don't think either Suraj or Chintan wants to lose his job," he said, pulling the straps of her bra down her shoulders, exposing her creamy breasts to his avid gaze. The tips were red from all the attention they had received from him yesterday. "Do they hurt?" he asked, tracing his thumbs over the nipples caressingly.

Kiara's eyes glazed over as she gave herself up to his caresses. "Not much. But they are begging for your kisses, can't you see?"

He reached out to close his mouth over a tip and drew his tongue over it. The next minute, he pushed her off his lap and got up, pulling her bra back in place and buttoning her shirt. "This is not going to work. Let's go to my place."

"Don't you have work to do?" Kiara asked him, thrilled to see the determined expression on his face.

"Nothing as important as making love to you. Come."

And she went, no questions asked.

Later in the afternoon, Kiara sent Arjun and Mudit a mail regarding her work. "I have all the evidence in place. Let's meet when you guys have time."

They met at five, which was the only time both men were free. Kiara quickly made a presentation, showing them the money trail, how it had left the coffers of the Mathur Group of Industries, moving from one account to another across three states before finally reaching the account of Patel Industries set up in a remote village in Uttar Pradesh. The total amounted to a little more than twenty-five crores in the span of five years before Arjun took over as managing director of the company. In the beginning, the transfers had been smaller amounts; as if the thief had been testing the waters. But it had increased more and more, obviously as he gained confidence. The last major transfer was four crores at one shot, four crores, twenty-three lakhs, seventy-seven thousand, five hundred and twenty-eight rupees to be exact. He was smart that way. It had always been an odd figure.

"In the last three years, for whatever reason, Kirit Patel has managed to transfer only a few lakhs at a time, the total amounting to less than one crore." Kiara concluded her presentation.

Mudit looked at Arjun. "The transfers must have reduced speedily after you came on board, Arjun. That's how it comes across to me."

"I knew it!" Arjun jumped to his feet, gnashing his teeth. "You're right, Mudit. That must have been the reason. But this is simply ridiculous. How dare he steal money from the company he has been working for? The bastard! I'm going to kill him."

"You don't need to soil your hands with his blood," said Kiara. "All you have to do is contact the cyber cell. I know Inspector Sanjay Mehra and have worked with him on many cases. Sanjay Uncle would trap your man before he even realises what hit him."

"What do you say?" Arjun asked Mudit who was quietly listening to the other two.

Mudit shrugged. "I'll go with Kiara's suggestion. Let's call the cyber cell and get the man arrested."

"Kiara, will you call Inspector Mehra?" Arjun asked her.

"Right away."

Kirit Patel had disappeared into thin air!

He had called in sick at the company and hadn't been in from the day Arjun had thrown him out of his finance director's post. The police found a nephew, Harish, at Kirit's Andheri flat.

"Where is Kirit Patel?" Considering the high-profile nature of the case and the kind of money involved, Inspector Sanjay Mehra personally conducted the interrogation.

"Kirit Uncle has gone on a holiday with Asha Aunty. At least, that's what he told me. I, personally, think he's gone for some kind of a treatment. He's not been keeping well recently." Harish lowered his voice to give his two cents.

"What do you think is wrong with him?"

"High blood pressure. He has a heart condition."

"Where has he gone for this holiday-cum-treatment?"

"America. Hahaha! Where else?" Harish was enjoying himself, thrilled to be in the limelight for once in his life. As for being brought to the police cyber department to be questioned, he wasn't too bothered. It was his uncle they wanted to talk about and it had nothing to do with Harish himself.

"America is a big country, young man. Can you give me an exact answer to the question?" Sanjay was growing impatient. It looked like a waste of time, questioning this idiot. "Which part of America has your uncle and aunty gone to?"

Harish was flummoxed. It hadn't struck him to ask the same question of his uncle. When Kirit said that he and his wife were going to America for a while, he had simply nodded in response. After all, it was an opportunity of a lifetime to live in the 3BHK apartment which had a live-in cook and servant. Harish wasn't going to question Lady Luck who had simply breezed into his life. "I don't know, sir. He said America and nothing else."

"You may leave. And listen, don't leave Mumbai. I might need to question you again."

Harish gave the Inspector a firm nod before stepping out, his shocked eyes falling on Kiara Bakshi. What was she doing here? And of course, he recognised her after all these years. How could he not? She was the most beautiful woman he had dated, after all. Had the police arrested her for something? Maybe he could help, now that he was a rich man. Harish was sure by now all his uncle's wealth was already his. Kirit Patel had ensured his Will was documented, signed, and sealed under the aegis of Advocate Prakash Shinde. It never struck Harish that the Will could be changed any number of times as long as Kirit was alive.

"Hello Kiara." Harish walked over to her with a smile on his face, his stride confident. "How have you been?"

She shrugged, running her eyes over him. What the hell had she seen in this man? The expression in his eyes were shady, giving her the creeps while his chin was so weak. Yuck! "Hello Harish. I'm good." She didn't bother to ask him how he was. She just wasn't interested to know.

"How's your father? Has he recovered from his loss?"

Kiara rolled her eyes. The question was coming ten years too late. "He survived," she said briefly before turning towards the door when Arjun walked in.

Harish's eyes went wide with horror when he recognised Arjun Mathur, the head of the Mathur Group of Industries. How did Kiara know him?

"Hello, sir, Mr Mathur," said Harish, hoping to ingratiate himself to his uncle's boss. He was sure Kirit would thank him profusely for his gesture.

Arjun looked at the other man with a deep frown on his face. He hadn't liked the familiar way he had been talking to Kiara. "Do I know you?"

Harish gave Arjun a big smile, putting his hand out. "I'm Harish Patel, Kirit Patel's nephew. You know, your finance director Kirit Patel. He's my father's cousin."

"Hmm." Arjun noticed Kiara bend her face to hide a grin. It was obvious Harish had no clue as to his uncle's status—the lack of it—in Arjun's company. "Well, let me tell you that your uncle doesn't work for the Mathur Group any longer. It has been a while since he was dismissed." He took Kiara's hand and walked into Inspector Sanjay Mehra's office, not noticing Harish's mouth fall open in shock.

But… but it was only the other day when Kirit had told his lawyer he was still working in the Mathur Group of Industries. Harish had been there at the meeting in Advocate Prakash Shinde's office.

What the hell was happening here?

She lived with her parents and he didn't really think it was possible. But he was desperate enough to ask her anyway.

Come over

Eh? Sure?

Of course. Don't u dare get cold ft now

See U in 20

Arjun jumped off the bed to pull on a pair of shorts and t-shirt before thrusting his feet into his sneakers, pocketing his keys before rushing out of his flat. Wasn't it a good thing there was no traffic in the middle of the night? He was at her bungalow gate in twenty-five minutes flat.

Placing her overnight bag in the back seat, Kiara got into the passenger seat to throw her arms around his neck and kiss him soundly on his mouth. "I've missed you."

"Not as much as I've missed you," he declared, crushing her against his chest and returning her kiss with equal fervour. "Let's get home." He reversed the car and drove off as if the devil was on his tail.

Kiara had left a message for her parents that she was going out for the weekend with some friends. Well, they weren't very fussy and it wasn't the first time she went out late at night. She planned to stay back with Arjun over the weekend, unless he had a serious objection.

She leaned her head on his shoulder, unable to resist rubbing her cheek against him. "Any news about Kirit?" she asked. She had stopped going in to Arjun's office once the report had been filed.

"Nothing so far. You know he's run away to America. But they haven't found out where exactly. It was a good thing you tracked down the money when you did. They managed to block his account just in the nick of time. Two more days and everything would have disappeared into a foreign account. It might have taken years to prove our case against him and get the money back."

"That bad?"

"Yep." He turned to press a quick kiss on the top of her curly head. "Thank you, sweetheart."

Kiara giggled. "You aren't planning to get away with simply a kiss, are you? Let me tell you upfront that you can't."

"Hahaha! I haven't driven all the way in the middle of the night to give you a smooch. Get it?"

Kiara gave an exaggerated sigh, rubbing her nose on his arm. "I want to take a bite off you. I wanna…"

Keeping an eye on the rear-view mirror, Arjun suddenly shifted the car to the last lane and brought it to a stop. Snapping off their seatbelts, he pulled her into his arms to kiss her deeply. "They have a law against drunken driving. Shouldn't they have something about driving along with an ardent girlfriend?" he growled as he bit into her earlobe.

"Am I your girlfriend?" she asked in a breathless voice, looking up into his eyes.

"That's a dumb question." He bent down to nip her collar bone. "Of course, you are." One more sharp nip of the other earlobe. "Why do you ask?" He turned his head to take a bite of her luscious lower lip. "You don't think I am your boyfriend?" He lowered his head to bite the curve of her breast. "Tell me."

Kiara was gasping for breath, caught between the sweltering passion and her runaway sense of humour. "Arjun! Stop it. This is too public a place. You don't want a hovering policeman to catch us in a compromising position, do you? Let me go."

"Only if you promise to keep your hands to yourself and your mouth shut," he threatened mockingly.

"I was only…"

"Kiara!" He took her hand and placed it against his rock-hard shaft. "Have some mercy on me. I've been going around like this for four days."

"Ouch!" She caressed him, giving him a final kiss before moving away. "I promise to behave."

It took all of three minutes before she peeped at him from under her eyelashes. "Can't I make verbal love to you? I wanna…"

"Shut your trap, woman. Unless you want me to fuck you right here in the middle of the highway." Arjun growled, clenching his jaw.

"Hmm… okay." She eased back on her seat, watching the scenery as he drove swiftly, swearing under his breath.

He pulled her out of the car and into his arms when they reached the parking lot. "I took half as much time reaching your home," he grumbled, nuzzling her neck.

"Are you saying you find me a distraction?" she asked, giving him an innocent glance.

Throwing her bag on one shoulder and picking her up bodily, he walked towards the elevator bank. "I'm not going to answer that question."

Wrapping her legs tightly around his lean waist, Kiara lay her head on his broad shoulder, giving a sigh of pleasure as the lift carried them to the tenth floor. They never reached the bedroom before he was inside her on the living room couch, still half-clothed as they sated their senses desperately, both coming swiftly and simultaneously.

"Kiara…" Arjun pressed hot, steamy kisses across her face and neck, his hands on her bare waist as he pushed her top further and further up before he encountered the lacy bra which held her breasts in place. "I want all of you."

Getting up to pull her top and bra off in one swift movement, she lifted her breasts in her hands to offer them to him. "So, take me."

With a long groan, he buried his face in her breasts.

How he had missed her the past few days! It hadn't taken long for Kiara to grow under his skin. But he was too scared to use the L word. Of course, he didn't for a minute think Kiara was after his wealth. She was the only child of a multi-millionaire businessman and was also wealthy by her own rights. And the bill for her stint at the Mathur Group of Industries, though well deserved, was massive.

But there was still something which stopped him. The sense of betrayal he had felt at Jane's hands had cut too deep and made him totally wary of women.

Though he could see Kiara was different, most definitely.

What touched him deeply was the way she was an equal partner in bed, giving as much as she took. She couldn't have been more different from Jane on that count. How he wished he could wipe Jane's memory off his mind forever?! But it dogged him every time he looked at another woman, making him hate the whole species.

But Kiara seemed to be changing all that. Were they meant to be together? While the week had been a busy one, he had still missed her terribly. Her voice, her touch, her softness, they all kept him grounded, he realised.

Was he in love? There! He had voiced the L word, even if it was only in his head.

He lifted the sleeping Kiara and carried her into his bedroom, placing her gently on the bed and lying next to her. He spooned her back to his front and cuddled her, a hand cupping her breast, relishing the softness.

With a soft sigh, Arjun shut his eyes and went to sleep.

It was close to noon when Arjun woke up. A smile automatically transformed his face when he saw the sleeping Kiara next to him, her tumbling curls all over the pillow. Pressing a gentle kiss to her cheek, he got up, his stomach growling in hunger. Checking his phone, he saw there was a missed call from his mother.

"Hey Mom, how have you been?" Arjun asked cheerfully as he added the coffee granules and water to the electric coffee maker before switching it on.

Anjali was startled to hear her son sounding so cheerful. She couldn't recall him sounding so happy, not in many years. "I'm good, Arjun. I was wondering if you can come home for lunch. And bring Kiara along if you can."

Arjun was confused for a minute. How the heck did his mother know Kiara was with him?

"Do you think she will come?" his mother asked when there was no reply forthcoming from Arjun.

It looked like his mother's invitation had nothing to do with Kiara's presence in his apartment. With a broad smile, Arjun said, "I'll ask her, Mom. I'm sure she would love to come."

"Perfect. I don't suppose you know her food preferences, do you? I'll let Parth decide what to make for lunch."

"Do my preferences count at all?" asked Arjun, tongue-in-cheek, as he removed the ingredients for a double cheese omelette from the fridge.

Anjali laughed gaily. "I don't know, you will have to ask Parth that. Here, he wants to talk to you."

"Parth, hello."

"Hey Arjun. So, is the lady coming over for lunch with you?"

Arjun shrugged. "Let me ask her first."

"Somehow, I don't think she's going to refuse you."

"Hmm…" said Arjun, munching on a breadstick hungrily, "and you could be right."

"What gives?" asked Parth, unable to miss the joy which brimmed over in his stepson's voice.

"I think I'm in love." The words kind of burst forth from Arjun. He couldn't help recalling how much Parth had gone through with him during the Jane fiasco. He was sure the older man would be happy for him.

"With Kiara?"

"With Kiara."

"Congrats Buddy. I'm truly happy for you." Parth was so glad Arjun was finally free of Jane's clutches. It had been so long.

"Don't mention anything to Mom yet."

"You know something? Your Mom is going to murder us both for keeping secrets from her. It was only on Sunday I…"

"…told her all about Jane and my suicide attempt?" Arjun's expression turned wary as he wondered what his mother must be thinking of him. "Should I stay away today?" he asked, before laughing loudly when sudden mirth overtook him. His mother was a softie and absolutely adored him.

"Don't be an idiot." Parth laughed as well. "We will expect both you and Kiara. What do you want for lunch?"

"I will take anything, Pop, served with your love," said Arjun in a soft and emotional voice.

"That I promise, Brat, as always." Parth was equally emotional. It seemed like the young man he knew so long ago was back, all thanks to Kiara.

Arjun entered the bedroom ten minutes later with a tray in his hands. Hearing the flush turn in the bathroom, he placed the tray on a small table which he set on the bed. Turning, he opened his arms to Kiara and was absolutely thrilled when she rushed into them.

"Good morning, my Kiara." Arjun kissed her deeply, tangling his tongue with hers.

Kiara kissed him with equal enthusiasm before pulling out of his arms. "I need that breakfast. Shall we have a go at it first?"

He grinned. "Are you sure? I thought we'll make love." He reached out to grab her breast and squeezed it.

Kiara groaned. "Food! I need the energy boost before another bout of sex," she grumbled.

"Okay, if that's how it is. You obviously prefer the food over me."

"Meh!" She poked her tongue at him before sitting on the bed in front of the table, her legs crossed, not at all conscious of her nakedness. "Come fast if you want anything at all," she said, forking a piece of egg into her mouth. "Mmm… this is so delicious. Don't tell me you made it? Or is your cook here?"

Sitting next to her, Arjun caught hold of her hand as she took a piece of toast to her mouth and turned it towards his face to feed himself.

"Arjun! I'm hungry," she grumbled, reaching for another piece of toast.

"So am I," he said, folding a piece of omelette in a slice of bread. Dipping it into the ketchup, he fed her a bite before popping the rest into his mouth.

Kiara promptly moved over to sit on his lap. "Just so you find it easier," she said, her eyes dancing mischievously.

Arjun thoroughly enjoyed feeding the two of them before pouring the coffee from the flask into two mugs. "Cheers!" he said, touching the tip of his mug to hers.

"Cheers!" She leaned back on his bare chest and sipped from her coffee mug. "This is heaven."

"Are you sure?" He whispered cheekily into her ear. "I was planning to show you a slice of heaven *after* breakfast."

She turned around to press a soft kiss on his rough cheek. "You are my heaven." There, she had said it.

Let him make whatever he wanted to out of it. Kiara was overwhelmed by her feelings for him and didn't plan to hold herself back. If he didn't care for it, too bad.

"Kiara..." Arjun placed his empty mug on the table before taking hers and doing the same. He placed the table down on the floor before turning to her. "I... we need to talk."

She gave him a wary glance. That wasn't exactly the response she had expected from him. "Aren't we going to make love?" she asked, her voice gruff with emotion. She was suddenly scared and wasn't sure if she wanted to hear what he had to say.

"We will, but we need to talk first."

She gave him a small nod, feeling bereft when he moved away from her to settle back against the bedhead. Quickly, she pulled the comforter over her body which had suddenly gone cold, waiting for him to speak.

"I was barely eighteen when I met Jane at Kingston University. I was in love; totally, completely, insanely in love." Arjun's gaze was fixed on the far wall and he didn't notice Kiara turning pale as the colour completely drained from her face.

He sounded so passionate and so much in love. How the hell could she compete with his love for a ghost? Arjun obviously had this Jane installed on a pedestal and worshipped her. Shit! Kiara moved to lean against the bedhead too, but kept as far away from him as possible. She bit her lower lip hard to stop herself from crying out when she noticed the pain on his face.

"We spent all our free time together till a point came when we couldn't stay away from each other. That was when I bought an apartment and invited her to move in with me. She was from a poor background and worked in a restaurant to support herself. How much ever I offered to support her, she refused and insisted on standing on her own feet. I couldn't help admiring her for her independence and fell all the more in love with her."

If he mentioned his love for 'the ghost' one more time, I'm going to walk out of his home. That's a promise!

"There were a number of small things I recall now. All I can say is I was totally blinded to her faults. I never noticed how she always called the shots, even the times when we had sex. She was a selfish lover. I became aware of that only after meeting you, Kiara."

When the hell is he going to end this torture? Does he really think I'm interested in the ghost?

"We were together for a year and a half when one day I got a call saying she had met with an accident, dying on the spot. I'm sure you can imagine how I felt. I was heartbroken. I…"

Despite herself, Kiara reached over to take his hand in hers, gently stroking the back, feeling terrible for his sake. "Yes, Arjun. I can imagine. I'm so sorry for your loss," she said in a soft voice, lifting his hand to press a kiss to his palm.

Arjun was shaking his head, a bitter smile on his lips. "That's not the whole story."

What more can there be?

"I was simply shattered when I found out Jane was actually running away with Peter, our senior at college. They were going to get married that day. She had been at the wheel when the accident happened. Peter escaped with a few scratches, but lived to tell the sordid tale."

"Oh my God!" Kiara's eyes went wide in shock as she placed both her hands over her mouth, staring at him. "Don't tell me." She wanted to pull him into her arms and hug him close. But he was obviously not finished, not yet.

"In a moment of madness, I went back to my flat and slit my wrist." Arjun spoke the words in a rush as if to get them speedily off his chest. He had never spoken about the incident to a living soul, not after confessing to Parth and having his stepfather jump down his throat.

"Oh Arjun!" Kiara threw away the comforter to go to him, her arms around him even as she rubbed her hands down his back. "I feel you, Arjun, I feel you," she said, pressing soft kisses all over his face.

"You don't think I'm a coward?" he asked in a choked voice, overwhelmed by her hugs and kisses.

"No, my darling. You were little more than a teenager at that time. And that woman… that woman, I would have killed her with my bare hands if I had ever met her."

Startled laughter burst forth from Arjun, a feeling of lightness filling him as he pulled her close to his chest. "My Kiara, my love."

"Am I?" She still felt jealous of the 'total, complete, insane love' he had felt for the ghost.

"Yes. I love you." Sensitive to her feelings, he continued, "It's not the love of a teenager, but the love of a fully-grown man. I love you from the bottom of my heart, my Kiara. Will you be mine?"

"Let me see. I have a few conditions," she said, her black eyes dancing with mischief as she gazed into his glowing brown ones.

He squeezed her bottom with both his hands. "Go on," he said, a dangerous sparkle in his gaze.

"I need you to feed me breakfast in bed, every morning."

"With my own hands, yes."

"I need you to make love to me twice a day on an average."

"Done, even if it kills me."

"Hmm… you can kiss my feet… er… once a day should be good enough."

He lifted her foot to kiss the instep. "Now will you be mine?"

"Mmm…" She studied his face mischievously. "I suppose I will. Though I might make more conditions as we go along."

That earned her a slap on her bottom. "That's for having a smart mouth. What do I get in return, you little minx?" he asked, nibbling her ear.

"Let me see." Kiara counted on the fingers of her left hand; her face serious for a change. "You have my undying love, my complete loyalty, and the most exciting partner in bed. Will that do?"

He pushed her on the bed and climbed over her. "What more can a man want?" he growled against her throat before making love to her thoroughly.

Just as they were about to leave for lunch at Anjali's home, Inspector Sanjay Mehra called on Arjun's cell. "Hello, Inspector Mehra."

"Hello, Arjun Mathur! Is it possible for you to come over to the cyber cell now? This won't take long. I'm planning to call Kiara over as well."

"Sure, sir. I can do that. And don't bother to call Kiara. I'll bring her along with me."

"Righto, then. I'll see you both."

"You heard me," said Arjun to Kiara before calling his mother. "Listen, Mom. I'm going to be late. Something urgent has come up. I'm really sorry about this. Will you please tell Parth? I'll probably get there in a couple of hours. And don't hold lunch for Kiara and me, okay? Just in case we are delayed."

"Oh!" Knowing her son, Anjali was sure it must really be something urgent. "Okay. You take care. I'll tell Parth."

"See you, Mom."

"You're bringing Kiara, right?"

"Yes, Mom."

"Good. See you both soon, bye."

"Ahem! It's a good thing our lunch has been postponed. I need some clothes, Arjun," said Kiara when they got into the elevator.

"Why? What's wrong with what you are wearing?" He ran his eyes from the top of her curly head to her feet encased in open-toed shoes. "You have the sexiest legs I've ever seen," he said, throwing an arm around her slender waist.

"And how many have you seen?" Kiara asked, giving him a saucy grin. "Which is also exactly why I need a change of clothes. This dress is simply too short for lunch at your mother's place."

She was wearing a red and white dress—with spaghetti straps—which stopped at mid-thigh. While it was perfect attire for a weekend at one's boyfriend's home, it definitely wasn't one she would want to meet his mother and stepfather in.

"You want to go shopping. Sigh! Okay," he grinned, taking her hand in his as he walked swiftly to the parking lot.

"Yep," She responded as she slid into the passenger seat. "What did Sanjay Uncle want?"

"He didn't tell me. Just that he wanted to meet you and me as soon as possible. And by the way, my mom wanted to confirm you were also going over for lunch."

Kiara gave him a brilliant smile. "I like Anjali Aunty and Parth Uncle. Talking of which, let me speak to my parents too. You must come over for dinner sometime next week."

"Whoa!" Arjun pretended to loosen the collar of his cotton shirt. "Suddenly, everything seems to be on fast track."

For a moment, Kiara was startled, before she saw the teasing smile on his face. "Isn't it? Arjun Mathur gets himself a girlfriend." She lifted her hands to draw a rectangle in the air as if she were reading the news headlines.

"Believe me, it's truly worth celebrating." He leaned over to give her a peck on her cheek just when the signal turned green. "Today's shopping's on me and no argument."

Kiara shrugged, laughing. "Mum's the word. Who's arguing?"

They got out at the cyber cell office at the Bandra Kurla Complex and had to wait for a few minutes before the Inspector got free. Kiara noticed someone waving and turned to see Harish sitting in one of the chairs in the waiting room.

"Hi Kiara."

She gave him a regal nod before turning back to Arjun.

"Why is that guy after you?" Arjun asked her, frowning. He hadn't liked it the other day either when Harish had greeted her in this same office.

"You remember I mentioned this guy who dumped me because my father became pauper?"

Light dawned on Arjun's face. "Kirit's nephew Harish Patel is *that* Harish. Do you want me to take a swing at him?"

Kiara giggled. "Mwah! My hero. Thanks, but no thanks. He's simply not worth it." She got up to walk with him towards Inspector Mehra's cabin when a policeman beckoned to them.

"Come in, come in," greeted Inspector Sanjay Mehra, ordering tea for the three of them. "Kirit is not on holiday but has flown the coop, just as I had thought all along. I only wish it were possible to find out which city he's in. I don't have the funds to have my men run all over the US of A."

"His nephew still doesn't know?" asked Arjun. "Has he spoken to Kirit any time recently?"

"They seem to chat almost every day. I even told Harish to ask for Kirit's whereabouts. But while the nephew is an idiot, the uncle is too cunning." Inspector Mehra was thoroughly irritated that the case wasn't moving forward.

"Hey, I have an idea. Can I have a look at Harish's phone? The one he's getting Kirit's calls on?"

"I can get it for you, of course." Inspector Mehra lifted the intercom and gave some instructions to an assistant.

A few minutes later, a policeman walked into the office to hand over a smart phone to Inspector Mehra. Before anyone spoke, Harish walked into the cabin as well. "Why do you need my phone?" he asked, an angry frown on his forehead.

"You can't simply barge into my office, Harish Patel. Get out and stay out." Inspector Sanjay Mehra ordered in a soft but firm voice.

"But your man took my phone."

"Of course, he did, because I asked for it. Didn't he tell you so?"

Harish looked sheepish. "But I'm bored. You insisted that I wait. What will I do without my phone?"

"Go for a walk or a hike, maybe. You'll get your phone back in ten minutes."

"What are you going to do with it?"

The Inspector got up to bang a fist loudly on his desk. "I'm conducting a criminal investigation, damn it! I don't need to explain my actions to you. Now get out, unless you want me to boot you out of my office. Should I?"

His face red, Harish fled.

Kiara took the phone from the Inspector and quickly opened it. It took her but three minutes to trace the whereabouts of Kirit's phone. "He's in Boston."

Arjun's eyes went wide in admiration while Inspector Sanjay Mehra gave a bark of laughter. "Why the hell did I not ask you to do it sooner?"

"Hahaha! All the best, Sanjay Uncle. Can we leave now? We are getting late for a lunch appointment."

"Of course." He shook both their hands. "This should get sorted in a week, max, Arjun. Not to worry."

"Thank you, Sir."

They quickly stopped at a shopping mall in Hiranandani Gardens where Kiara bought a cotton knee-length skirt in kalamkari print of black and orange paired with a short matching sleeveless top. Changing into them in the trial room, she did a pirouette in front of Arjun. "Works?"

"So well that I've gone rock hard," he whispered passionately in her ear.

Colour flared on Kiara's cheeks. "Arjun! Behave! We are going to meet your parents." She gave him a mock glare.

He gave her a wink, taking her elbow and walking to the car. In the end, they managed to reach Parth's apartment by 3 pm.

"Sorry Parth," said Arjun, giving his stepfather a hug.

"Shut up, Brat," said Parth. "Hello Kiara, welcome. So glad you could make it."

"Hello Parth Uncle. I wouldn't have missed this for the world. How have you been?" Kiara gave him a wide smile, thrilled when he pulled her into a hug as well.

"I'm good, *Beta*. Come along in. I'm sure you guys must be famished."

Arjun hugged his mother before taking Kiara's hand and pulling her forward.

"Hello Kiara. I am so glad to see you again," said Anjali, hugging the younger woman. She had been amazed by the change in Arjun. He looked so cheerful and carefree. It was obviously all thanks to this young woman.

"Anjali Aunty!" Kiara hugged her back with equal enthusiasm before whispering in her ear, "You have the most wonderful son."

Anjali gave Kiara a wide smile. What more could a mother ask for from her son's girlfriend? She affectionately pinched Kiara's cheek. "Come, let's have lunch first."

Lunch was simple fare with *veg biryani, dal tadka* and *kachumber raita* along with fried *papad*. There was also *iced tea* and *masala chaas* to go with it.

Conversation flowed smoothly as they spoke about their diverse careers, each one in an entirely different space. They all had common interests in reading and watching films. They decided to go for a film during the coming week.

"Everything's so delicious, Aunty." Kiara complimented wholeheartedly as she took a second helping of the *biryani* and *raita*.

"You should thank Parth for it. He's the chef in the family."

Kiara turned to give Parth a wide smile. "Your cooking skills are even better than your writing skills, Parth Uncle," she said.

"Hahaha! Thanks, I suppose." Parth went in to bring the strawberry shortcake he had baked with fresh strawberries. He sliced it and served the pieces on four dessert plates.

"My favourite! Thanks, Parth," said Arjun, handing a plate to Kiara before picking one for himself.

Kiara spooned a piece into her mouth and wasn't really surprised when it melted away. "I'm speechless, Uncle. Don't be surprised if I land up for lunch every weekend," she threatened mockingly, mischief dancing in her eyes.

"You are welcome," said Parth and Anjali simultaneously, laughing out loud when Parth blew his wife a kiss.

For the first time, Arjun didn't resent his mother's and stepfather's closeness as he turned to give Kiara a small wink.

"Here, please have this. I'm too full," said Kiara, offering the last bite of her cake to him.

Arjun took her hand and guided the spoon to his mouth, looking deeply into her gaze, forgetting they weren't alone. He wasn't aware of the older couple watching them avidly.

Anjali's eyes were shimmering with unshed tears as she met her husband's. What a relief! Arjun was so obviously in love with Kiara and she with him.

On Monday morning, just as Arjun poured the beaten eggs into a frying pan, his phone rang. It was his aunt Smita. "Hello Smita Aunty."

"Arjun *Beta*, how have you been? I hope I'm not disturbing you. I should have called you during the weekend, but I was too caught up with things. You know how it is after a wedding in the family and all that."

"That's okay, Aunty. I'm good. How are you? You must be so tired after all the work which comes with arranging a wedding."

"Tell me about it. Phew! It was really hectic, the past six months, running from pillar to post getting everything together. But now things are calmer. Why did you not come for the reception? I was so eagerly waiting for you along with a number of friends who were keen to make your acquaintance."

"I'm sorry about that, Aunty. I had to go to another wedding." Arjun's lie came out glibly, as he had no guilt about skipping the reception. There was no love lost between him and his father's family. He couldn't stop being irritated about the way they treated his mother, without any respect.

"Oh! That's why you didn't come. I understand and forgive you. Listen, I wanted to actually talk to you about something really important. That girl who was there that day… I think her name was Kara or something like that, I fail to recall. She…"

Arjun gritted his teeth, praying for patience. Now what? "Go on, Aunty. What did you want to speak to me about?"

"I think she's a loose character. I thought it's best to warn you. Nowadays *na*, the girls are so bold and ready to do anything to catch a boy in the marriage market. You know that Kara who was hanging all over you on Sunday; she was dancing with Mudit all the time during the *Sangeet*. Can you imagine? Flirting with one man on Saturday evening and with another man on Sunday morning. *Baap re!* What a loose character! I thought it's best to tell you. You are such an innocent boy, Arjun, just like your father. But these girls nowadays *na*? They are simply too much."

"*Ho gaya?* I need to go, Aunty. I'll catch you some other time." A furious Arjun cut the call before his aunt could say anything in response.

Kiara had left early in the morning and here he was getting ready to go to work. What a beginning to what looked like a terrifically hectic week?! Arjun had lost his appetite. Throwing the egg and toasted slices of bread on the plate he kept for the crows on the kitchen window sill, he quickly got ready and left for work, his bad mood colouring his whole day.

"Are you working from home today?" Chandresh asked Kiara, folding the newspaper and keeping it aside to focus on his daughter and breakfast, in that order.

Kiara shrugged. "I'll probably take the day off is what I am thinking," she said.

"Is everything okay?" asked Chandresh, surprise on his face. The Kiara he knew insisted on working all seven days of the week. And just now it looked like she had returned from a weekend out with her friends.

Kalpana came to sit at the dining table, watching her husband and daughter chat, not joining in. Worry was eating into her. Her daughter was all of twenty-seven and wouldn't let her parents look for a suitable husband for her. Nor would she find her own husband. Tch! What was with this modern generation?! The mother was totally frustrated.

Kiara gave her father a broad grin. "Everything is fine, Papa. In fact, things couldn't be better. I just finished a project with the Mathur Group and it was totally successful."

"I'm sure you made a pretty packet from it," said Kalpana, unable to hold back the irritation on her face.

Kiara turned to her mother, astonished. "Of course, I did, Mama. Shouldn't you be happy, instead of being angry about it?"

Kalpana gave a huge sigh, her plump figure shuddering in the aftermath. "What's the use of all that?" she asked. She felt it was because of her rocking career that Kiara was refusing to be tied down to a husband. And for Kalpana, the ultimate success for a woman was to get married and have kids.

"Mama!" Kiara shook her head. Her mother would never understand what Kiara's career meant to her. "Maybe what I am going to tell you might make you happy. Maybe!"

Chandresh grinned as he munched on a piece of *mooli parantha*. "It's about a man," he guessed. "Are you in love?"

Kiara's face flamed a fiery red as she smiled at her father. "How did you guess, Papa?" She got up to hug him. "Yes, Papa. Arjun Mathur is…"

Chandresh hugged his daughter back, a warm expression on his face. "Will that be the managing director of the Mathur Group?"

"You know him?" Kiara asked.

"Not personally, no. Why don't you invite him home for dinner? Today or tomorrow? Kalpana, what do you think?"

Tears were pouring down Kalpana's cheeks. She hadn't been able to believe her ears when her daughter finally admitted to being interested in a young man. Finally! Finally, it looked like Kiara was going to get married. "I think it's a good idea. Why don't you call him, Chandresh? It's only right, instead of Kiara's casual invitation. What about his parents?" Kalpana asked Kiara.

"You both meet him first, Mama, before bringing his parents into the picture. By the way, his father is no more. His mother, Anjali, is married a second time to Parth Bhardwaj. So, Arjun has a stepfather."

Kalpana grimaced, not liking the information one little bit. "Married a second time?" she said, wrinkling her nose.

"Mama! Please don't be so judgemental. If Anjali Aunty married a second time, it's her business, surely?"

"Have you met this Arjun's mother?" Kalpana asked, not happy with this new turn of events. How could Kiara simply go and meet the man's mother? Without a by-your-leave from her parents? This new generation! Bah!

Kiara sighed. "Please Mama. The world has changed a lot. Nobody's so formal these days."

"All that is fine for talks. When push comes to shove, no one has changed in reality. Mark my words. They will want a dowry and a grand marriage at our expense. In the same old school style as our generation. *Kyun ji?*" Kalpana turned to glare at her husband as if it was all his fault.

Chandresh gave his wife a pacifying smile. "Kiara is our only child. What does it matter if they ask for dowry or not? What we have is all hers."

Kiara kissed the top of her father's head. "Arjun is too rich, Papa. I don't think he really needs our wealth, yours or mine for that matter. And Mama, I think you're worrying unnecessarily. You meet Arjun first and then you tell me what you think."

"Do you have a picture of his?" asked Kalpana, sniffing. She liked to be in control of every situation, at least at home. Now, it looked like things were snowballing too fast for her to wrap her mind around them.

Kiara went and hugged her mother. "Don't be so anxious, Mama. Arjun is a very nice guy. You meet him and judge for yourself. And no, I don't have his picture." Only selfies with him which were too private to be shared with her parents. "Shall I check with him if he's free today or tomorrow evening?"

"You do that, Kiara. I can't wait to meet your young man." Chandresh was all encouragement.

Kiara sent Arjun a message on WhatsApp:

My parents would like to meet you. Are you free for dinner today? Or maybe tomorrow?

The ticks remained black for twenty-four hours with no response from Arjun. She called him a few times, but he didn't take her call. Nor did he call her back. When she called him again in the evening, his phone was switched off.

She decided to wait the night out, just in case he was too caught up with something. After all, hadn't he messaged her in the middle of Friday night? Maybe he would message her late at night.

But there was nothing from him until the next morning. "So, when did Arjun say he will come to meet us?" Kalpana asked her daughter first thing at breakfast.

Slowly, Kalpana's gentle nagging got on Kiara's nerves. And at the end of it all, Arjun had neither pinged her nor called her till now.

Not one to be easily shaken, Kiara was stunned into thinking that Arjun was maybe not speaking to her. What else to think? She knew he was a busy man. But couldn't he find a few seconds to ping her at least?

What must have gone wrong?

There was only one way to find out. She quickly got ready and rushed out of her home to get into her car. Only to find her way blocked by the car which was entering the compound.

Arjun! It was Arjun's BMW, with him at the wheel.

Kiara jumped out of her own to rush towards him just as he parked his vehicle and opened the door.

"Kiara! Sweetheart!" He pulled her tightly into his arms before kissing her deeply. "Where are you off to?"

"I was going to your office. You didn't see my message nor did you answer my calls. I didn't know what to think. I…"

He pressed his mouth to hers once again in a torrid kiss. "I know. I'm sorry about that. I lost my phone yesterday and I've still not found it. It was late when I finished at work yesterday. Without a phone, I feel so stupid and lost. Mudit had also left or I would have taken your number from him. That's why I'm here, first thing, before I take off to shop for a new phone."

"Ouch!" Kiara couldn't help grinning even as she exclaimed, throwing her arms around his neck and offering her mouth for another kiss which he delivered with fiery passion.

"I've missed you, sweetheart," he whispered in her ear, his hands running through her thick curls which crackled against his palms. "Will you mind if we get married ASAP? I don't think I can live without you."

Kiara's eyes shone up at him even as she nodded vigorously. "I say YES. Why don't you come in and meet my parents?"

"As long as your father hasn't loaded his gun to shoot me for kissing his daughter senseless in the view of all your neighbours."

Kiara hooted with laughter. "Let's go find out," she said, holding his arm as she dragged him into her home.

"Papa, Mama, see who's here."

Chandresh walked out of the dining room to see the strapping young man, tall and handsome, holding his daughter's hand in his. "Hello, Arjun. Welcome to our home," he said.

Arjun took the hand offered by Kiara's father even as she introduced, "This is my father, Chandresh Bakshi."

"Hello, sir. Nice to meet you. May I call you Chandresh Uncle?"

"You must. Come along. You must have some breakfast with us."

"I wouldn't mind as I didn't have the time to stop for a meal."

Chandresh lifted an eyebrow, amusement in his dark eyes. "Why, was there an emergency?"

"But of course. I misplaced my phone and had no way of contacting Kiara and vice versa."

"Aah! No wonder." Chandresh gave his blushing daughter a knowing look. "Kalpana, see who has come. This is Arjun Mathur, Kiara's young man. And Arjun, this is Kiara's mother, Kalpana."

"Hello Aunty, lovely meeting you. Now I know where Kiara gets her beautiful looks from. She looks exactly like you." Arjun gave Kiara's mother an engaging smile as he reached forward to touch her feet before hugging her.

That Kalpana was floored was putting it mildly, having been rendered completely speechless.

As the talk went on to organising a quick wedding, there was no argument from Kiara's mother who had decided by now that the sun rose and shone out of her son-in-law-to-be.

Which made life easy all around. Arjun and Kiara hired an event organiser to put together a wedding in two weeks' time, just the *muhurat* on a Sunday evening for which a hundred and fifty select guests were invited.

Smita and Nandita were dumbfounded when they saw who the bride was. To begin with, they were flabbergasted to know that Kiara was the only daughter of the super-rich Bakshis. They had heard of the family via friends and knew the daughter was not only extremely intelligent and qualified but also ran a successful business of her own. So much for them assuming that she was a flirt, who was on the lookout for a rich man to marry.

Not one to admit being wrong, Smita said, "You know something, Nandu. I knew they were perfect for each other the minute I set eyes on them together."

Not to be left out, Nandita said, "You are absolutely right. And our Arjun is not a fool. He's not one to be taken in by some cheap flirt. Otherwise, how will he run the multi-million business which our dear Jayant had set up?"

The bride and groom, resplendent in their wedding attire, had eyes only for each other. They tied the knot by Punjabi rites at 1.30 am as Anjali, Parth, Kalpana and Chandresh watched on emotionally.

"You guys owe me a special treat," said Mudit, laughing as he hugged both Kiara and Arjun in turn. "But for me, you wouldn't have met."

"Meh!" Kiara poked her tongue at her best friend, her eyes shining with mischief and joy.

"Most definitely, Mudit. I definitely owe you one." Arjun hugged his friend, feeling too grateful. On a lighter note, he teased, "Should I maybe start searching for a life partner for you?"

Kiara burst out laughing when she saw the startled expression on Mudit's face. "Serve you right," she told him.

Mudit shook his head in amazement. The grim Arjun he had gotten used to over the past decade seemed to have disappeared for good. "You've really worked magic on the man, Kiara," he told her on an aside.

Kiara turned red on hearing her friend's words. "All I wish for is his happiness."

Mudit nodded. "God bless you both!"

It was finally past four when the last of the guests left and the wedding couple could go to their honeymoon suite.

"Mrs Mathur." Arjun lifted her in his arms before stepping into their suite, his honey brown eyes glowing with love as he looked down at his gorgeous wife's face.

"Hmm." Her arms around his neck, Kiara lifted her face for his kiss. "I love you, my Arjun."

"And I love you, my Kiara."

With the help of the cyber police in the United States, Inspector Sanjay Mehra had Kirit Patel arrested for fraud and brought back to India. A case was filed against the ex-finance director of the Mathur Group of Industries for cheating the company of more than twenty-five crores of rupees.

It was a watertight case with all the evidence in place and there was simply no way for Kirit to escape the law. He was sentenced to jail for ten years. Luckily for him, the sentence wasn't longer as the money had been recovered, all thanks to Kiara's timely investigation.

While Advocate Prakash Shinde brought forth a number of arguments in his client's favour, nothing held good against the solid evidence of the money trail left by Kirit.

"Bad luck!" shrugged Prakash as he watched his client being taken away to jail. Kirit's wife Asha and his nephew Harish stood back watching the man being taken away, tears in their eyes. While Asha was shedding tears of sadness, Harish's tears were full of anger and disgust.

It was all because of his uncle that Harish had quit the job he had been holding on to for fifteen years. And here he was, penniless and with the extra responsibility of taking care of his aunt by marriage.

Adding insult to injury was the fact that his ex-girlfriend was happily married to the one whom Harish considered his arch-enemy, the one who was the cause of his uncle landing behind bars, the billionaire businessman Arjun Mathur.

Some people are born with all the luck in the world! Harish fumed, utterly frustrated. It never did strike him that his lack of purpose and sheer laziness had placed him in the soup he was in.

While Kirit swore vengeance on Arjun Mathur and cursed the man a million times, he had no choice but to kick his heels in prison as he grew old and frail. It never dawned on Kirit that he was but suffering for his own greed, the greed which had led him to steal Arjun Mathur's hard-earned wealth; money which had never belonged to him.

While both Kirit and Harish heaped abuse on Arjun's head, neither had a clue as to the role played by the ethical hacker who had gathered all the evidence against Kirit.

Arjun threw a special party for an intimate group of guests in Kiara's honour. While the world presumed it was to celebrate their marriage, only those present—Chandresh, Kalpana, Anjali, Parth, Inspector Mehra, Mudit and Krish—knew the truth. Kiara was a true heroine and Arjun appreciated her more than ever.

"To my heroine!" Arjun raised a toast which was highly appreciated by those present. Kiara grinned widely as she leaned on her new husband's arm, her black eyes sparkling with pride and joy.

EPILOGUE

Kiara traced the white line inside Arjun's left wrist, the mark from the time when he had slit it all those years ago. The years before Kiara; the years which had been a penance for him.

They were on their honeymoon in Mauritius, both having turned brown with all the swimming and sunbathing in the last five days.

Just now, they were stretched lazily on a deck chair, Kiara lying back on her husband's chest as they sipped from colourful fruit cocktails. They were at the back of the villa Arjun had hired for two weeks, watching the sun go down over the Indian Ocean.

"Does it bother you?" asked Arjun, his large hand spread over her flat abdomen as he hugged her close to his warmth.

"What?" she tilted her face up to his to ask him lazily.

"The mark on my wrist, the evidence of my suicide attempt."

She shook her head, her curls tickling his chin, making him smile. "I'm not bothered about that. But yes, there is something about the whole thing which disturbs me."

He sat up straight, seating her between his legs. "Spit it out, now."

With a soft sigh, Kiara admitted what had been in her mind from the day he had spoken to her about Jane. "You must have really loved her, right? You felt so deeply for her that you wanted to kill yourself, all because she died. I suppose I'm a bit jealous. I know it's stupid to be jealous of a ghost, but," she shrugged, "in a way it makes my life more difficult. If it were a real, live, breathing woman, I could have simply plucked her eyes out. But now, there's nothing I can do. I..."

"Kiara!" Arjun lifted her small chin with his hand, making her look up into his eyes. "Did I hear you right? Are you seriously jealous of Jane?"

She gave a nod, an earnest expression on her face. "Please forgive me. I'll get over it for sure. Though it might take time."

Arjun shook his head. "But what are you jealous of? Jane never loved me. And as for my feelings, I was in love with an imaginary woman who never existed. Slashing my wrist was more of a..." He searched deep within for the right words before continuing, the words flowing in a torrent, "...more of a punishment to myself, for placing my faith in someone who didn't deserve one little bit of it. Anger was my foremost emotion. I was angry with myself, with the world, for having been dealt with such terrible cards. To have landed with someone who didn't care for me at all and who was a cheat into the bargain. I wanted to do something, break something, punish somebody. There was only me and I did the only thing I could think of doing at that time. You know, I had to take some action, or I might have simply exploded; such was my anger." He reached over to kiss her soft cheek. "Are you able to understand what I am saying? I was in love with a mirage. There was no real person. The woman who died in the accident wasn't the woman I loved. There is only one woman in this world whom I have fallen in love with and she's sitting right here in front of me." His voice was a passionate whisper by now as he brushed his lips against her ear. "You are my one and only love, Kiara."

There were tears in Kiara's eyes when she looked up at her husband. She could completely understand his emotion and even more so, his words. A soft smile lit up her face, making it glow in the twilight, her black eyes shining with her love for this man who had come to her all broken. He was completely mended now. And was she glad Arjun's Penance had kept him in hibernation and out of the reach of other women, until the time they had been brought together by providence!

"And you are my only love, my darling." Kiara took his hand and placed it on her breast.

Arjun needed no further encouragement as he unclipped her bikini top and threw it down on the sand before cupping her lush breasts in both his hands, squeezing them adoringly, his thumbs stroking the turgid nipples.

Kiara threw back her head to relish his touch, her hands on his bare thighs as she mewled her pleasure. She gasped when she felt his mouth close over a breast, lifting her hands to wrap them around his head to hold him in place as she pressed herself closer.

Arjun suckled both her breasts in turn, laying her down on the deck chair before climbing on top of her, reaching a hand to run a finger down the seam of her vagina, thrilled to find her so hot and wet. He untied the knots at the sides of her bikini bottom before pulling it from under her. It joined her top and his briefs which were already lying on the beach.

Kiara rubbed a damp tongue over a flat male nipple, taking a small bite of his sensitive flesh, making him jump.

"Do that again," he invited, his voice a succinct growl as his manhood tautened further in reaction.

Kiara stroked her tongue over his other nipple, repeatedly, before taking a bite of it, thrilled to feel him shudder in her arms. Her hands gripped his strong shoulders as he rose up to pull her legs around his lean waist before gently pushing his penis inside her feminine core and settling deep inside with a grunt. Soon, he began to ride her, first slowly, then fast, up and down, and up and down before they came together so explosively that it was a long while before they could catch their breaths.

Arjun fell on her, apologising profusely. "I'm sorry. Just give me a minute to get my breath back and I'll get my weight off you."

She held on to him tight, her arms crossed at his back. "You're going nowhere. I like your weight on me only too much."

Arjun couldn't help laughing at his wife's fervour as he pressed his lips to her forehead in a soft kiss.

"My precious Kiara!"

THE END

OTHER BOOKS
BY
SUNDARI
VENKATRAMAN

AN
Autograph
FOR ANJALI
SUNDARI
VENKATRAMAN
AMAZON BESTSELLING AUTHOR

At thirty-nine, Anjali Mathur feels like an exotic bird trapped in a golden cage, hating the life of the idle wife of a multi-millionaire husband who simply has neither the time nor the inclination to give her his attention.

She meets Parth at a common friend's party. It's not just his looks that Anjali's attracted to, but his gentle and understanding nature.

At forty-two, Parth Bhardwaj is an internationally famous author, writing under a pseudonym. Always having steered clear of married women, he has a difficult time keeping away from Anjali, feeling drawn to her from the moment he sets eyes on her.

Just when the two finally realise that they are meant for each other, the unthinkable happens.

Jayant Mathur is found murdered in his bed, making both Parth and Anjali the prime suspects.

Will Anjali ever find happiness in her lonely life?

SUNDARI
VENKATRAMAN
AMAZON BESTSELLING AUTHOR
MEGHNA

The young and dashing Rahul Sinha lives in England with his parents, Shyam and Rajni. He is an only son of the rich banker. Rahul is totally attached to his father but does not care for his mother. Read the book to find out why….

Rahul is exulted with his efforts at work paying off and plans a holiday with his best friend Sanjay Srivastav who lives in Mumbai with his wife Reema, kids Sasha and Rehaan and most importantly, his sister, Meghna. Rahul recalls meeting Meghna just before they parted six years ago.

Meghna works for a website and also teaches modern dance as she loves it. She's thrown for a toss when Rahul comes visiting. She had thought he had forgotten them.

But how could Rahul do that? Sanjay's his best friend and Rahul had always treated their home as his own. Sanjay's mother had been more of a mother to Rahul than his own. Rahul had stayed away after moving to England or so Meghna believes.

Thus begins the story of Rahul and Meghna, the teasing, the flirting, the anger, the tears…

…will they find love?

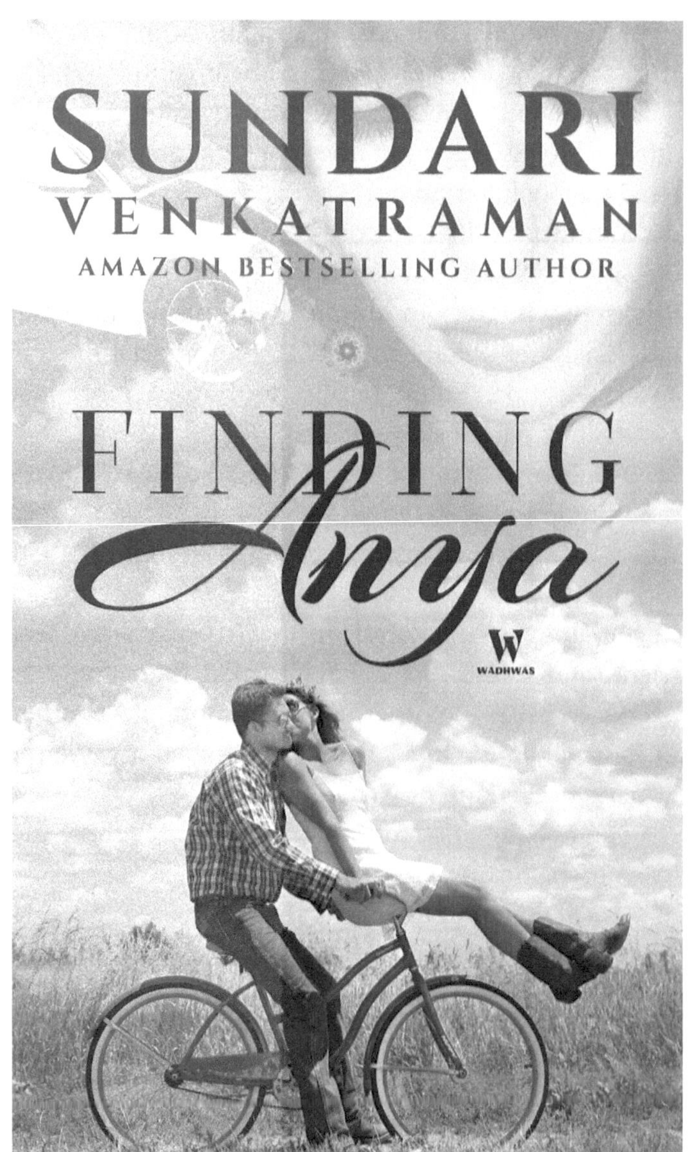

SUNDARI
VENKATRAMAN
AMAZON BESTSELLING AUTHOR
FINDING
Anya
W
WADHWAS

nya Chhabria wakes up in a hospital room with no recognition of who she is and where she belongs. In her troubled times, Anya finds her anchor in a handsome stranger. But is he really unknown to her?

Dev Wadhwa's past finds him when he sees Anya lying unconscious in the middle of the road. Not willing to let go of her one more time, Dev takes her to the hospital and later to his farmhouse, where he helps her recuperate.

Sparks fly and Dev and Anya fall for each other! But the feisty Anya refuses to commit herself to marriage as her loss of memory looms larger than life.

Things aren't easy with an ex-husband, not-so-understanding parents, and a jealous neighbour thrown into the mix. What if Anya's memory never comes back?

Will Dev and Anya get a second chance?

Or will circumstances force them apart, yet again?

Connect with Sundari Venkatraman here:

Sundari Venkatraman Books

Sundari Venkatraman Books

https://www.sundarivenkatraman.in

Author Sundari Venkatraman

@sundarivenkat

@sundarivenkatraman

sundarivenkat@gmail.com